M000099180

LIVING LITERATURE:
The CLASSICS *and* YOU

TELECLASS
STUDY GUIDE

Governors
State
University

Copyright © 1996 by Governors State University

ISBN 0-7872-8475-0

This guide is protected by copyright. No portion may be reproduced
for any purpose without permission from Governors State University.

All rights reserved. No part of this publication may be reproduced,
stored in a retrieval system, or transmitted, in any form or by any
means, electronic, mechanical, photocopying, recording, or otherwise,
without the prior written permission of the copyright owner.

Printed in the United States of America
10 9 8 7 6 5 4 3 2

LIVING LITERATURE: *The* CLASSICS AND YOU

TELECLASS STUDY GUIDE

Jeffrey Lynch

Associate Dean, College of Arts and Humanities
Eastern Illinois University
Charleston, Illinois

Sponsored by:
Board of Governors Universities

Member Institutions are:
Chicago State University
Eastern Illinois University
Governors State University
Northeastern Illinois University
Western Illinois University

Produced by
Governors State University
University Park, Illinois

KENDALL/HUNT PUBLISHING COMPANY
4050 Westmark Drive   Dubuque, Iowa 52002

CONTENTS

INTRODUCTION

Introduction and desired outcomes

It is tempting for me to cast the purpose of a course like ours into the kind of chiseled-in-granite language that one finds on the side of libraries—the course will introduce you to many of the primary literary texts that have shaped Western culture into the twentieth century, will challenge you to see your place within that culture and to think critically about it, and will demonstrate the vitality of "classic/canonical" texts which articulate the premises of that culture. And while I do believe that the course will do all these things, I don't believe that these are the main reasons for taking it.

The main purpose of the course, as I see it, is to give you pleasure—the kind of fund, if you will, that comes from reading good literature and then thinking and talking about it. It is a uniquely human pleasure, of course, that will come readily and easily to some of you, perhaps more grudgingly to others. And please rest assured that it is a pleasure that can be learned. It takes neither a genius nor a gift for languages to learn it—as countless generations of readers can attest. Indeed, look around the teleclass participants and see and feel the enthusiasm for reading and discussion that these adults have developed over a lifetime. The so-called "Great Books" are accessible to every college student who has learned how to read. Quite simply, you don't have to be an English major to read and talk about literature.

One of the things you'll notice about our readings is their seriousness. By that I don't mean that they are solemn or deadly earnest—some are very funny, even slapstick. But all attempt to say something important and memorable about what have proven over time to be important human issues: the problem of identity (am I made in the image of God or am I a dung beetle?); the problem of codes and values systems (shall I live by a warrior ethos or shall I cultivate my garden?); God and religion; illusion and reality; war and violence; love and hate; gender and class, to name but a few. These are all issues that we wrestle with on an almost daily basis.

Finally, I see two desired outcomes for a course like ours, both having to do with the self. If this course works for you, you should come to the end of it with an enlarged sense of self. You will take into yourself through the imagined circumstances of "fictions" a wide variety of experiences—vicarious experiences, to be sure, but real nonetheless. It is to have your awareness as a human being enhanced and sharpened without having to experience directly the events imagined. For example, after reading The Death of Ivan Ilych you will know very well what it is like to die. You will feel the alienation of the dying, the terrible isolation, the unmitigated aloneness, the fear and terror that confronting one's own mortality entails. And you will be changed in subtle ways—perhaps with a more heightened sense of compassion for the terminally ill, perhaps with a close examination of the kind of life you are currently leading.

Each selection you read in this course should change you in some way and to some degree. At the very least you will come to a more intimate understanding of a portion of reality. In the process you should realize the second desired outcome of the course: you should come to a better understanding of yourself. At its best, a course like ours is a kind of introduction to the self, as we see ourselves reflected in the various characters we meet in the readings. Sometimes we will admire what we see, sometimes we will cringe in recognition. Rarely will we fail to make the connection. Good literature does not end in the reading. It becomes a source of thinking, questioning, and evaluating. It is not an escape from life but a part of life, both the writer's and the reader's. You will be fortunate, indeed, to carry around with you as part of your intellectual and emotional landscape such inner companions as Homer, Sophocles, Virgil, Dante, Shakespeare, Moliere, Milton, Voltaire, Goethe, Flaubert, Dostoyevsky, Tolstoy, and Kafka. They will stand you in very good stead.

Required readings

All the texts except one in this course are contained in the following:

Mack, Maynard ed. <u>The Norton Anthology of World Masterpieces</u>. Vols. 1 and 2, 6th. Ed., New York: W. W. Norton and Co., 1992

The one exception is Dostoyevsky's <u>Crime and Punishment.</u> This is readily available from libraries or bookstores. I recommend the Modern Library edition.

How to use this Study Guide

This Study Guide is intended to help you get the most out of the lessons on the videotapes. The videotapes capture the discussions I conduct on each work with those taking the class. You will notice that the direction of the discussion is often influenced by the interests of my audience. As with any good discussion, we journey together. I would like you to journey along with us, to feel that you are in a seat along with the other class participants.

Try to follow a fairly disciplined order in studying this course. First, of course, read the text: you will find the reference to the Norton anthology at the beginning of each chapter. Read the text as if you were reading it for the first time. Write observations in a reading journal - there are blank pages in the guide for this purpose. Jot down questions as they occur to you while reading. Ask yourself repeatedly why you think the culture has considered this particular text so important. What does it tell us about ourselves?

After reading the text, I suggest that you read the corresponding chapter in the Study Guide. It contains an introduction I have written for each work, a synopsis of the highlights on the videotape, the names of any special guests we might feature, and a commentary on the discussion. If you read this commentary before you watch the tape, you will find that it will function as an advance organizer for you, helping you to stick the discussion elements on the pegs you will have made for them in your mind's eye.

After you have watched the tape, consider the review questions I have written. Whether you write responses or just think about them, you will find that they will help you to synthesize what you have read and heard on the tapes. I have also included a brief list of other books for further reading about the works we have discussed.

Acknowledgments

I would like to acknowledge with thanks the stimulation and assistance I received from the participants in the class. Over the few short weeks we were together we developed a warm relationship in our own journeys of exploration. The participants are:

Barbara Campbell	Mary McGinnity	Yvonne Daubenspeck
Ada Middleton	Joan Hayes	Eric Nicholson
Luke Helm Jr.	Helen Obuch	Phyllis Janik
Peter Pantarotto	Chadwick Jumao-as	Virginia Parker
Patricia Koutouzos	Charles Shields	Elaine MacKenzie
Rosemary Tassio	Agnes March	Susan Vorwerk
Barbara Marshall	Valeria Wolff	

Finally I would like to express my thanks for their cooperation to the faculty and staff of the:

Division of Humanities and Social Sciences

College of Arts and Sciences

Governors State University

Dr. Sonny Goldenstein, Chairperson

LESSON 1:   GENESIS, CHAPTERS 1–3

 Before you read this chapter of the Study Guide

READ: Text: Maynard Mack, Ed., Norton Anthology of World Masterpieces,
          vol. 1, pp. 49-53
          All the introductory material, especially "Masterpieces of the Ancient World" (pp. 1-10)
          "The Old Testament" (pp. 45-49).

As with all texts in this course, try to read the text as if you were reading it for the first time. Write observations in a reading journal or in the margins of the book. Jot down questions as they occur to you while reading. Ask yourself repeatedly why you think the culture has considered this particular text so important. What does it tell us about ourselves?

I. INTRODUCTION

Bereshith. The first word of the Hebrew Bible denotes a concept so large, so bewildering, so almost beyond our imagination's ability to contain it and give it shape that it almost defies our comprehension. Yet it is a good place, I think, to start a course like ours— "In the beginning."

With a single word the Book of Genesis seizes the imagination of every reader, yet it does so in language so sublime in its simplicity and unadorned directness that it remains to this day one of the masterpieces of world literature. To read the Bible as literature will perhaps prove difficult for some of you, since many of you will come to it after years of uniquely religious interpretation. As far as you can, I ask you to put that religious overlay aside and read the stories of creation and paradise as human stories written down by people to be read by people for what they tell us about our own humanity.

The bulk of the stories in Genesis, the end product of centuries of honing and refining, had long been told orally before they were written down—the motifs of creation and a lost paradise, for example, can be found in various forms in the myths and legends of Israel's neighbors. Folk tale, legend, myth and reliable history (and much of Genesis is reliable) all come together to form the stirring narrative of humankind's attempt to come to grips with its own nature and the nature of its God.

I think you'll find the video interviews with Dr. Maynard Mack, Professor Emeritus of Yale University and editor of The Norton Anthology of World Masterpieces, and Dr. Willard Gaylin, a practicing psychiatrist and psychoanalyst, president of The Hastings Center and author of Adam and Eve and Pinocchio: On Being and Becoming Human, most provocative and stimulating. Each speaks eloquently of the particular vitality of literary "classics" to remind us of our essential humanity.

II. VIDEOTAPE SYNOPSIS

Lesson 1 examines the creation stories of Chapters 1 and 2, with special emphasis on the differences of language, style, conception of deity and purpose. It examines the question of what it means to be made in the image of God. The discussion of Chapter 3 focuses on the enduring vitality of the Adam and Eve story, the Myth of the Fall. Do Adam and Eve assert their basic human dignity in their defiance? What does it mean to be fully human according to the Adam and Eve myth? Why should the gaining of knowledge and experience and the loss of innocence and simplicity acquire a connection with sin, error and pain?

Video interviews with:

Professor Maynard Mack, Yale University, Editor of <u>The Norton Anthology of World Masterpieces</u>

Dr. Wil Gaylin, Author, <u>Adam and Eve and Pinocchio: On Being and Becoming Human</u>

III. VIDEOTAPE COMMENTARY

Note to Students: I suggest you read this "Commentary" section before you watch the videotape. You'll find that it will help you organize your thoughts in a more useful way than if you were just to watch the tape "cold." When you have finished viewing the tape, read this section again.

A. *Opening class discussion*

I begin with some introductory remarks for the course, asking the question: Why should we spend our valuable time discussing literary works that were written, in some cases, thousands of years ago? I received some varied responses from the class:

Ada suggests that it is like getting acquainted with old friends. She read the classics when she was young and now finds that she has the time to read them again. Similarly, Phyllis read them when she was "younger and more naive" and wonders how they will now be different. Valeria hopes that reading the books will give her insights into both the works themselves and into herself. She endorses Socrates' dictum that "the unexamined life is not worth living." She speculates that dialogue with a group will offer her more than she would get from isolated reflection. Although you will of course not be able to take part in the discussion directly, I hope that by listening to our conversations you will come to feel that you are part of the discussion group.

Barbara C., who grew up in rural Nebraska where she did not read the classics, offers the example of her two sons—one of whom read the classics in school and the other of whom did not. Barbara believes that this has caused a significant difference between the two. Another student believes that if these works have survived through the centuries, there must be some enduring truths in them.

I conclude the introductory material on a personal note: I normally teach these works to a class of 18-22 year olds. This class, however, brings a wealth and a variety of life experiences to bear on the individual texts, which should prove both stimulating and provocative to me and to them. As Barbara M. remarks, "We are all teachers learning from each other.... Here we'll talk about things that we don't talk about in our everyday life."

B. *Interview with Professor Maynard Mack*

I ask Professor Mack the same question I asked the class: why read these works? He suggests that we read them to enlarge the boundaries of the self. By reading them we vicariously experience some essential human emotions and experiences. And in doing so, we extend ourselves. Great literature is always about us, about the self.

C. *Class discussion of Genesis, Chapters 1 and 2*

The form of Genesis 1 is ordered, highly structured, formal and formulaic. It generates answers to some basic questions about the world around us and about how things first got to be. The force behind it all is God. We are made in the image of God, which makes us the crown of creation. Created nature and animals are below us on this hierarchical scale of being. We are to have dominion over them. The God of Chapter 1 is an utterly transcendent deity, unseen and formless. He simply speaks and it is done. The language of Chapter 1 is simple, direct, precise, repetitious and orderly to enhance the theme of God as the great orderer of the cosmos. Try reading it aloud to hear the effect.

When we move to Chapter 2, we immediately notice differences. The God of Genesis 2 is an anthropomorphic deity who walks in the garden in the cool of the day. He learns things through inquiry and dialogue. He even experiments, creating Adam first and then seeking a "help meet" for him, finally creating Eve. Notice that the creation story in Chapter 2 lasts only a day, that the order of creation is different and, indeed, that the key to creation is different—both involve water but in one the water is potentially destructive and must be held in check by a firmament while in the other the water brings life to a parched soil. Perhaps the most significant difference, however, is in the matter of language. Chapter 2 gives us a freer, looser, picturesque story with plot, character and dialogue.

What accounts for these differences in style, language and conception of deity? Note that even the names for God are different, "Elohim" (translated as "God") in Chapter 1 and "Jahveh" (translated as "Lord God") in Chapter 2. Biblical scholars have long held that there are several authors of Genesis and that the two creation stories are separated by centuries. Genesis 2 is the earlier of the two, written ca. 950 B.C., during the reign of David. He is known to us as "J" (after "Jahveh "). The author —or, more likely , a group of authors—of Genesis 1, writing in the 6th century B.C., is known to us as "P", the priestly writer. Notice how "P" condenses the eight days of the ancient Babylonian creation story to six in order to accommodate the story to the traditional six day work week plus the traditional Sabbath. Significantly, "P", the priestly writer, regards the Sabbath as not only embedded in the creation but also as the culmination of the creation.

J's masterpiece is the temptation in the garden, Genesis 3. Indeed, it might be argued that, considering its simple brevity, the story in Chapter 3 of Genesis carries more weight per line than any other literary text one can think of. From a literary point of view, the story of the Fall offers a rich variety of dramatic characters, situations and themes. It raises questions about the relationship of human beings and God, humans and Nature, humans and evil, humans and their past, and, of course, man and woman. It allows speculation on the nature of: evil, guilt, innocence, experience, knowledge, shame, sin, authority and freedom, among others.

Genesis 3 tells an archetypal, mythic story—the inner journey from innocence to experience. It is knowledge that caused the Fall. We could all write our own personal story of our Fall.

Adam and Eve's eating from the tree leads to a discussion of the concept of good and evil and the concept of freedom and autonomy. One of the consequences of the Fall is a terrible sense of alienation for Adam and Eve. They are alienated from God (they attempt to hide from Him), from one another (they are ashamed of their nakedness; Adam blames Eve) and from the entire creation (the ground is cursed).

Peter suggests that freedom will enable you to choose, although your choice could be a wrong one. Maybe the choice that Adam and Eve made was part of the divine plan. Adam and Eve act out the essential human drama. Temptation is a part of that drama. How are we to live with knowledge that causes such pain?

D. *Interview with Dr. Willard Gaylin*

I asked Dr. Gaylin how to read the Adam and Eve story and whether or not he thought it was not so much the story of the Fall but of a "Rise."

He suggests that you have to take the Christian gloss off the Jewish Bible. Christians promise Heaven, fusion with the perfect person, Christ. Jews weren't interested in that; they were interested in the species, not in individuals. God made them the chosen people. There is no salvation for an individual. It is very "communitarian." The Adam and Eve story is the birth of the human being, half

God's creature and half our own design. Dr. Gaylin doesn't see the Adam and Eve story as a Fall, but as a "Rise"—as the creation of human creatures with all our unpredictability. It certainly is the birth of morality. There has to be morality. William James said that if there were two people stuck on a rock, you would have a complete moral universe. The concept of a Fall may be a post-Genesis imposition.

Guilt, shame and pride support the concept of conscience. Guilt and shame are essential for the good human being. Responsibility is part of the joy and the necessity of being human beings. Exculpation has its limits. Not everything anybody does to another person is excusable.

I asked Dr. Gaylin whether or not he thought Adam and Eve were given a choice between security and autonomy. He replied that maybe they didn't have any idea what they were choosing when they chose. Responsibility did not exist at that point. Punishment was unknown.. The story, however, shows the power of human curiosity, human imagination and human hope. After Adam and Eve were kicked out of the garden, there's no despair at all. Instead, there's the renaming of Eve because she will be the mother of mankind. There is the assumption of a new life, a new birth, a new set of creatures. The story is about curiosity, about taking the punishment, and about maintaining optimistic hope for the future.

E. Final class discussion

I ask for responses to Dr. Gaylin's comments, asking such questions as: Are we better for our freedom to make moral choices? Is the concept of good and evil more relative than we would like it to be? Is the story about a "Fall" or a "Rise"?

Barbara M. sees it as a rise. God's plan was for Adam and Eve to eat from the tree of knowledge and to go on and start a new life. God knew human foibles. Valeria suggests that God knew that humans were unfinished products. God's image does not mean that we look like God. It is a spiritual concept, not a physical one. I end the discussion by saying that the story gives humans an extraordinary dignity, that we are set apart as something very serious and very different from the rest of creation. But it entails a special responsibility. What, finally, is the role of knowledge? Will it cause my ruin or will it ultimately make me in the image of God? ♣

Now, please enjoy the videotape.

IV. REVIEW QUESTIONS

1. How is the great creation account that opens Genesis structured and what views of the world does it express?

2. Compare the tone, style, language and content of the first creation narrative (the P account in Genesis 1:1-2:3) with those of the second account (the J account in Genesis 2).

3. What basic assumptions about such matters as the nature of God, man's relation to Him, the relation of the sexes, the nature of work, and the nature of good and evil does the story of the garden of Eden imply?

4. What is the significance of the fact that God forbids eating the fruit of the tree of knowledge? Why should the knowledge of "good and evil" be forbidden? Are there kinds of knowledge that it is risky for human beings to have?

5. What is the role of the serpent (the serpent has not yet become Satan as it will later for Milton)? Is the serpent a way of passing the buck—of saying it's not our fault?

6. What do Adam and Eve gain by eating the fruit? What do they lose? Do you feel they gained more than they lost?

V. FURTHER READING

Gaylin, Willard. Adam and Eve and Pinocchio: On Being and Becoming Human. New York: Viking, 1990

Pagels, Elaine. Adam, Eve and the Serpent. New York: Vintage Books, 1989

Lewis, R.W.B. The American Adam: Innocence, Tragedy and Tradition in the Nineteenth Century. Chicago: University of Chicago Press, 1968

Milton, John. Paradise Lost. New York: J.W. Lovell, 1866

Shaw, George Bernard. Back to Methuselah. New York: Brentano's, 1921

NOTES

LESSON 2:   THE BOOK OF JOB

 Before you read this chapter of the Study Guide

READ: Text: Maynard Mack, Ed., Norton Anthology of World Masterpieces, vol. 1, pp. 69-86

I.   INTRODUCTION

The <u>Book of Job</u> is generally regarded as the literary masterpiece of the Old Testament, having received the highest of praise through the centuries. Martin Luther, for example, described it as "magnificent and sublime as no other book of Scripture." Tennyson referred to it as "the greatest poem of ancient and modern times." Carlyle asserted that "there is nothing written, I think, in the Bible or out of it of equal merit."

As hyperbolic as these estimates might strike us, it is nonetheless true that our generation comes to the <u>Book of Job</u> with a similar enthusiasm. Perhaps no other century than our own has more called into question the traditional answers given to the problem of theodicy. A century which has witnessed Auschwitz, Hiroshima, the killing fields of Cambodia or Africa might well wonder aloud about the presence—or absence—of a just and all-powerful God.

We were very fortunate to interview two leading commentators on the Book of Job, Rabbi Harold Kushner and Professor David Clines. Each brings a particular expertise to bear on the text. Harold Kushner is the author of the best-seller <u>When Bad Things Happen to Good People</u> and David Clines of the University of Sheffield (UK) is one of the world's leading textual scholars of Job. Each provides a fruitful avenue for the first time reader into the very difficult and challenging <u>Book of Job</u>.

II.   VIDEOTAPE SYNOPSIS

Does innocent human suffering deny the concept of a just god? The discussion focuses on the knotty philosophical question of theodicy and on Job's personal evolution from despair to faith. How does orthodoxy, in whatever form, keep one from an authentic pursuit of meaning?

Video interview with:

Rabbi Harold Kushner, Author of <u>When Bad Things Happen to Good People</u>

Professor David Clines, University of Sheffield, Author of a critical text on the <u>Book of Job</u>

III.   VIDEOTAPE COMMENTARY

I suggest you read this section before you watch the videotape. You will find that it will help you organize your thoughts in a more useful way than if you just watch the tape "cold." When you have finished viewing the tape you may want to read this section again.

A.   *Initial classroom discussion*

The <u>Book of Job</u> is difficult, elusive and metaphoric. I begin by asking what we mean by the patience of Job, since the Job of Chapters 3 and following seems to be anything but patient. From the prologue, we know why Job is suffering, but he doesn't. He is a very good man, yet he suffers, which brings up the problem of theodicy: how can we explain the presence of an all-powerful, all-good, all-just deity when there is innocent suffering in the world? What is this book about?

Note the Satan character in the Book of Job. Satan can be a problem for those of you new to this text. Note that he is not the "Devil" of later literature but one of the "sons of God" (1.6)—some kind of heavenly court, if you will. His name means "the adversary;" perhaps he is a sort of loyal opposition. Watch for the transformation of this character in later texts—especially Dante, Milton and Goethe.

Job screams defiantly at God: How dare you? Where is the charge? I did nothing wrong. There is no divine justice. I will maintain "mine own integrity before you." His is an act of righteous indignation. His three "friends" who come supposedly to comfort him are, in fact, spokespeople for the orthodoxy of their day. They know how God works. They are spokespeople for the orthodox doctrine of rewards and punishments: if you are good, you will be rewarded in this life; if you are a sinner, you will be punished. Job is obviously suffering; therefore, he must be a sinner.

Valeria remarks that this is very different from Adam and Eve who took their punishment quietly. I ask if it means that I should forget organized religion and be true to my own perception of how things should be? Barbara M. suggests that Job is calling God accountable to man as man is accountable to God. I add that there seems to be some kind of creative spark in heresy. Susan says that Job never says that if this is happening to me, there's no God there. I suggest that the Book of Job is not really about the question of theodicy, the question of innocent suffering. That question is never answered in the Bible. There is simply suffering; it happens, and we have to deal with it. Perhaps the Book of Job is really about faith, maintaining a faith in the face of an orthodoxy that could crush you. It is difficult to do. Virginia speculates that Job does what he does because he has a personal relationship with God; it's a contract between the two. It's a living, personal faith.

B.   *Interview with Rabbi Harold Kushner*

Rabbi Kushner begins by summarizing the Book of Job. He says it contains three postulates: 1. God is all powerful, nothing happens without his deciding so. 2. God is completely good, he rewards good and punishes evil. 3. Job is a good person. You can believe any two by denying the third. The intellectual challenge of the Book of Job is deciding on which one of the three one is willing to sacrifice so you can affirm the other two.

The book begins with Job's belief that God is so powerful that he can ignore considerations of fairness. This is the belief that Job has to outgrow by the end of the book. Rabbi Kushner's favorite part is in Chapter 13, where Job says, in essence, that if God is indeed the kind of God that you are talking about, He respects my integrity more than He respects your flattery. The greatness of the Book of Job is the legitimacy of protest. It is religiously proper to stand up to God. The Book of Job is definitely optimistic. The world does not treat good people fairly, but the good people can make themselves accept that state of affairs through faith in God. It's a once in eternity concession to Job's innocent challenge. You and I could not pull it off. God would not come to speak to us. It is a radically anti-conventional book.

How does one look for signs of the presence of God today? The answer is not ontological or cosmological, but rather it is that we always see ordinary people doing extraordinary things. People find within themselves qualities of soul that they didn't think they had. The answer to tragedy is not to explain it, but to survive it. God's promise is not that the world makes sense, but that when the world is unfair He will be there to hold our hand and give us the means to be brave enough to go on living in an unfair world. Martin Buber once said that theology is talking about God, religion is experiencing God. The difference between theology and religion is like the difference between reading the menu and having dinner. Job's friends are reading the menu, they are telling Job about theology. Insisting upon God being behind every instance of violence, unhappiness and tragedy is the result of the desire to prove that what we have been taught in Sunday School is true. Job did not want a long explanatory talk, he needed understanding and affirmation of his faith in God.

C. Second class discussion

The Book of Job is so different from so much modern writing. Modern man experiences an overwhelming feeling of insignificance in the cosmic scheme of affairs, while Job was almost at the center of the universe. Knowing that someone is listening is a source of comfort. We both have the same dilemma, we are innocent sufferers, but at least Job feels that someone is in charge, whereas I don't. Is the Book of Job optimistic? Virginia says that to her the book says "You suffer, you come out and are rewarded." Job was rewarded. I suggest that Job moves through despair. As Dante said, "There is nothing worse than remembering former happiness in pain." It's a heroic journey. It's a battlefield of the soul. There are forces in the universe quite beyond anyone's control. Is Job you? Most of the class said, "Yes."

D. Interview with Professor David Clines

The Book of Job is an affirmation of the human spirit in the face of orthodoxy of all kinds. Job speaks of what he knows, and not what he speculates about. Speaking from experience against orthodoxy, he out-theologizes the theologians. Also, in our postmodern culture we have come to see that the question of closure, of wrapping things together, of finalizing them, and thereby achieving security and certainty is perhaps not the way this world is. There is no closure in this work. The Book of Job qualifies as one of the earliest postmodern works.

On the subject of how did the Book of Job end up being canonized in spite of its attacking orthodoxy in the Old Testament, Professor Cline takes what he calls a shallow view of canonizing. His belief is that canonization was not a matter of a group of holy people evaluating a book for its religious worth. He wouldn't be surprised if the canon of the Bible was more or less all the old books that we have. Books were in the canon because they existed. It is the reading public that decided on the fate of the book. The book would never have lasted if it didn't have a large reading public. He remarks that the huge irony of the work is that Job is laboring under a huge misapprehension that he is being punished for something. When in fact it was an experiment whose purpose was to see if a human being can suffer dreadfully and still believe in God. Job never knows why he is suffering. We, the readers know, but he doesn't. Just as the friends were all wrong, he too was completely wrong. Just as Job's fate is the result of God's wager with Satan, the whole book is a wager with the audience. It's the first seminar in history. Not even God finalizes the story, which is an amazing thing in a book of this character. In response to my question as to whether the book is optimistic or pessimistic, Professor Cline says it can be seen as either. "You can say: No matter what misfortunes befall human beings, there is something indomitable about the human spirit that perseveres. Or you can say no matter what comforts religion professes to offer to you, the fact is the world is in chaos and there is no meaning."

E. Final discussion

I end by saying that there are scholars who argued that this is a kind of early tragedy. I don't subscribe to this, in spite of it being a provocative argument. Tragedy is a less mature view of the world than comedy is. Tragedy is like an 18 year old, anguishing over the lack of the world's compliance with his views of how things ought to be. Tragedy is less mature than a comedic approach, which acknowledges the presence of tragedy, and finds it wonderfully funny, and absurd. I ask the class if Job is an idealist or realist. Valeria says that Jews are the chosen people, yet they are taught to suffer, in that sense the work is somewhat pessimistic. Phyllis says that it's a comedy in a Dante sense, more than a tragedy. Rosemary says that Job has a firm foundation to stand on, unlike those who threw in the towel. He has integrity. Orthodoxy comes from man-made rules, and Job was dealing with divinity directly.

I end by suggesting that we confront the orthodoxies we live our lives by. There are many, and they are difficult to confront. Works like the Book of Job enable us to confront them vicariously, which is easier. It is difficult to lead any kind of authentic life if your life is wrapped up in orthodoxies. The most provocative part of the Book of Job for me is that it ultimately forces you to question received and inherited opinion. What it forces upon us is to question tradition. Recognizing, questioning, and gaining authenticity in the face orthodoxy is a very difficult task for each individual. It takes courage and strength. The need for authenticity will be revisited again and again. ♣

 *Now, please enjoy the videotape.*

IV: REVIEW QUESTIONS

1. What is the Book of Job about, i.e., what is its theme?

2. What is the role of the prologue (chapters 1 & 2)? Does it diminish God's responsibility?

3. Recast in your own language the core of the arguments offered by the three friends. How do they differ from one another?

4. What is the source of Job's pain?

5. Does Job have a tragic flaw?

6. Consider the character of God in Job. How is He different from the God of Genesis? Is God a remote metaphysical force, inscrutable, powerful but not benevolent? Is the gap between God and man impassable?

7. How many kinds of evil does Job confront?

8. What is the view of human life—tragic, unbearably sad, futile?

9. What conclusions, if any, does Job reach—about life, about God, about himself?

10. Is the conclusion of the Book of Job inconsistent with the thought of the piece?

V. FURTHER READING

Kafka, Franz. The Trial. New York: Knopf, 1957

Kushner, Harold. When Bad Things Happen to Good People. New York: Shocken Books, 1989

MacLeish, Archibald. J.B. Boston: Houghton Mifflin, 1958

LESSON 3:   HOMER, THE ILIAD, PART 1

 Before you read this chapter of the Study Guide

READ: Text: Maynard Mack, Ed., Norton Anthology of World Masterpieces,
vol. 1, ~~pp. 92 - 124~~ 104-149
Homer, The <u>Iliad</u>   Books I, VI, VIII, IX

I.   INTRODUCTION

The transition from the world of the Old Testament to the world of Homer is a dizzying one. But like the Bible, Homer's <u>Iliad</u> serves as a foundation for the culture and literature of the Western world. <u>The Bible</u> and The <u>Iliad</u> formed the basic educational texts of the ancient Jews and Greeks, the books they considered, in different senses of the word, sacred. They have been revered not only as masterpieces of language and narrative but also as expressions of central truths about human beings and their place in the scheme of things.

The essence of Homer's epic is its careful depiction of the heroic world, especially the heroism that faces and suffers death. In many ways, Homer's world is a very alien one to a contemporary reader. The defining characteristic of the heroic outlook in <u>Iliad</u> is the pursuit of honor through action. The great man is one who, endowed with superior qualities of body and mind, uses them to the utmost and wins the applause of his comrades because he spares no effort and shirks no risk in his desire to make the most of his gifts and to surpass other men in his exercise of them.

His honor is the center of his being, and any affront to it calls for immediate amends. He courts danger gladly because it gives him the best opportunity of showing what kind of stuff he is made of. By prowess and renown he gains an enlarged sense of personality and well-being. By performing great deeds of valor he gains a second existence on the lips of men. Fame is the reward of honor, and the hero seeks it before everything else. Through it he becomes immortal, thus cheating death of its terrible finality.

The ultimate test of honor is human dignity. Anything that lowers it is dishonorable; anything that enhances it, honorable. Obviously, what results is a subjective system, since the concept of dignity is not precise and may well vary from man to man. In the last resort the only court of appeal is a man's own feelings. The hero is so sure of himself that he will not allow his final decisions to be dictated by anything but thought of his own honor. Thus, when Achilles is angered by an affront to his honor and refuses to fight for his fellow Greeks, it is futile for them to plead with him. Their needs are a far less cogent argument than his own sense of injury. Achilles fights not for his city, nor even for his fellow Achaeans, but for his own glory. He is an isolated, self-centered figure, who lives and dies for a private satisfaction.

No other character is as important as Achilles, and all center on him. The other warriors gain by contrast with him, particularly Hektor and Agamemnon, Priam and Nestor, Diomedes and Odysseus. As you read the epic, pay attention to how Homer individualizes each of his warriors. Notice, too, the role of women and the aged, friendship and family in this heroic world.

One final note on the gods. As Mack points out in his "Introduction to the Ancient World" (p.4), "The Greek conception of the nature of the gods and of their relation to humanity is so alien to us that it is difficult for the modern reader to take it seriously." Their role in the epic and their relationship to human beings is quite complex. Whatever else they are, they are utterly superior to human beings in both their power and their immortality—the two things these warriors crave most. Yet it is these very qualities, combined with their penchant for bickering and trickery, that make them less morally serious than the human beings under their sway. If nothing else, their presence in the narrative emphasizes the brevity of human life and the need for people to fashion some meaning out of their fleeting time on earth—even if it means dying well.

II. VIDEOTAPE SYNOPSIS

The class discussion focuses on the nature of epic, the tragedy of Achilles, the nature of the Homeric hero, the relation between humans and gods, and the nature of honor as a motivating principle. Discussion focuses on the <u>Iliad</u> as both a celebration of and a protest against war.

III. VIDEOTAPE COMMENTARY

I suggest you read this section before you watch the videotape. You will find that it will help you organize your thoughts in a more useful way than if you just watch the tape "cold." When you have finished viewing the tape you may want to read this section again.

I begin by establishing the context for the study of the <u>Iliad</u>. It will represent the Hellenic strain in western literature. The <u>Iliad</u> was meant to be heard rather than read. Within the first twelve lines Homer sets the subject and style of his presentation.

The next part of the discussion turns on the nature of the gods in the Greek world. The movement from the Old Testament to the Greeks is really a radical shift. Everything is on a large scale. The gods take us off the battlefield into their slightly less serious world. Remember the comic scene where Zeus is worried about Hera's (his wife) reaction to his solution of a given problem. We also discuss the relationship between mortals and gods. For example, is Odysseus helped by Athena because of his qualities or does he possess those qualities because she helps him? Helen's presiding goddess is Aphrodite. Helen knows that she is wed to a man who is her inferior. Man often seems to be a pawn to the frivolity of the gods. Rosemary says that what disturbs her is that there is no justice for man, that man is at the mercy of the gods. Certainly the gulf in power is unbridgeable. However, Hector is a free being in the <u>Iliad</u>. Achilles also makes his own choices, although he is destined to die. The women are the real victims. Phyllis questions the gods' power by saying that it depends in whose hands the power lies. I point out that tragedy is impossible without the possibility of choice. I refer the class to a powerful scene in Book 17 where Hera seduces Zeus during the third day of the battle, with the intention of changing the course of events. Zeus and Hera make love on a cloud, and then he falls asleep, and the tide of the battle changes. It is a painful scene, to see that in the midst of human suffering, gods entertain themselves while giving direction to events.

Another use of gods and goddesses is to objectify certain states of mind. An example is the fight between Achilles and Agamemnon in Book 1, where Agamemnon said I will return the girl, but I, being a king, can't go empty-handed, so I'll take your girl. Achilles pulls out his sword, and then Athena appears on the scene and stops him. Athena is the goddess of reason. This is a psychodrama objectified by the gods. Part of the fun of Homer is how he builds you up for a certain event and then he delays it, increasing anticipation.

Chad turns the discussion to Menelaus, asking where is Menelaus in all this. I reply that he is among the Greeks with Agamemnon, and he is a wonderful warrior. In Book 3 Menelaus and Paris meet on the battlefield. At that moment Homer picks up the entire past of the poem, the cause for the war. Aphrodite saves Paris from Menelaus.

We then move on to a discussion of the myths behind this epic. Probably the most significant of them is called the "Judgment of Paris." At Achilles' parents' wedding, the goddess of discord rolled an apple into the reception, inscribed with "to the fairest of them all." Paris has to make the decision as to whom to give the apple. Three goddesses are involved: Hera, Athena, and Aphrodite. Hera promises civil power, Athena promises him great military power, and Aphrodite promises him the most beautiful woman in the world. He chooses the most beautiful woman in the world, which happens to be Helen, the wife of Menelaus. Menelaus lets him in to his household, and Helen appears to have willingly left her husband and daughter for Paris, who takes her to Troy. In the second myth: the suitors for Helen's hand had vowed that no matter who won her hand, if the honor of that marriage were violated, the others would come to the rescue. A loose confederation is organized by Agamemnon, who has the most men, and he carries the scepter that traces its tradition back to Zeus. Homer just shows us a couple of weeks in the tenth year in the siege of Troy.

At this stage, Phyllis gives voice to the often-asked question as to why is the cause for the war always pinned on Helen when all these men had many other options? My reply is that given the world in which they lived, and the Heroic Code by which they lived, their options were limited.

The discussion now turns on the question of honor. Honor is gained by doing a great deed, not by leaving a great work. The enemy can and should be treated in an honorable way. For example, in Book 6 Andromaches talks to Hector about how Achilles killed all of her brothers and her father, whose armor and body he burned. But what she remembers is that he didn't defile her father's body. He treated his body with chivalry, with honor. Susan speculates that because their lives were short, honor gave them something to define their life with, which may possibly be able to put them above the gods. It gives their lives meaning. And she adds that they did value wisdom. People like Nestor and Odysseus were prized for that.

We now look at the message of the Iliad. I ask the question as to whether life seems futile as you look at the Iliad. The book ends on a remarkably powerful emotional note: the meeting of Achilles and Priam, and we are told that they will be given twelve days for the funeral rites of Hector so that they can burn and bury their dead, and then it's killing and death again. There is a great line there: as is the generation of leaves, so is the generation of men. Everything is destroyed, the men and the things. Troy itself is burnt to the ground.

Chad says that he has a problem with Achilles' promiscuity, that he slept not only with his "prize" but with other women as well. This is a nice introduction to the notion that women in the Iliad had symbolic value, and were not just bed mates, in that they represented all that the heroes thought was their due. Men control action and fate, women are pawns. Achilles doesn't settle for atonement, i.e. gifts of treasure and women. He wants revenge, as in the face of his short life, it is the revenge that provides a greater chance of gaining honor and fame. It is a greater deed. Susan points out that by refusing the material goods offered by Agamemnon, Achilles says that he cannot be bought, and that life is more important than the goods, what's more there is something more important than life, i.e. honor.

I end the discussion by saying that we confront in the Iliad something in our nature that we need to keep under control, and here is a world that gave it free reign. The kinds of values that are brought forth in warfare, the friendship, the love, the honor, empathy, constitute the beauty of war, if we can use such a phrase. But Homer also shows you the utter bestiality of it, the unrelieved horror and suffering. As we end the first hour, I muse as to whether we have really progressed. What do you think? ❧

 *Now, please enjoy the videotape.*

IV. REVIEW QUESTIONS

1. Discuss the concept of individual freedom and responsibility, i.e., to what extent are the decisions made by the heroes independent, individual decisions?

2. Discuss the statement (from the Introduction, p.4): "Morality is a human creation, and though the gods may approve of it, they are not bound by it."

3. The opening invocation states that the theme of The Iliad is Achilles' "anger." Is this an adequate description of the poem's theme? Might it serve as the poem's title?

4. The quarrel between Agamemnon and Achilles centers on captive women. Does this fact reflect the importance of women in the Homeric age or their unimportance? Is it a paradox that the Trojan war, though fought by men, is all about women?

5. What is the role of Diomedes in Book IX? Of Nestor? Is the demoralized Agamemnon the same man we met in Book I?

6. To what extent, if at all, is Achilles justified in rejecting Agamamnon's overtures in Book IX? Achilles' removal of himself from the fighting has often been called "sulking;" is this the right word, or the whole story? If Achilles is "proud," is his pride justifiable? Is he simply personally offended, or is he defending a principle? How does the matter of honor enter into all this? What, exactly, is honor in this context?

V. FURTHER READING

Dodds, Eric R. The Greeks and the Irrational. Berkeley and Los Angeles: University of California Press, 1951

Owen, E.T. The Story of the Iliad. New York: Oxford University Press, 1947

Schein, Seth L. The Mortal Hero: An Introduction to Homer's Iliad, Berkeley and Los Angeles: University of California Press, 1984

Willcock, Malcolm M. A. Companion to the Iliad. Chicago: University of Chicago Press, 1976

LESSON 4:   HOMER, THE ILIAD, PART 2

 ☞ **Before you read this chapter of the Study Guide**

Rᴇᴀᴅ: Text: Maynard Mack, Ed., Norton Anthology of World Masterpieces,
vol. 1, pp. 124 - 161 150 - 209
Homer, The Iliad   Books XVIII, XIX, XXII, XXIV

I.   INTRODUCTION

His anger with Agamemnon having run its course and having cost him his best friend, Achilles' passionate anger is now redirected to Hektor. Half-mad with passion, inflamed beyond all restraints Achilles proceeds to slaughter Trojans on a grand scale, culminating in his shameful treatment of the body of Hektor. His tragic fury finds no appeasement even in victory. Only after the funeral games for his friend, Patroclus, does Achilles regain his equilibrium. He gives back the defiled body of Hektor to old Priam, a fellow sufferer, and promises a truce of twelve days for Hektor's burial. For Achilles prowess in battle is the whole man; for Hektor it is only a part. Homer is very careful to surround Hektor with family and city. His courage is less instinctive than deliberate—he has to be brave, so he is. He knows he is fighting a losing cause, but he also knows that he has no alternative but to face his enemy. He is a brave man—despite his flight from Achilles—and he dies a hero's death, courteous and chivalrous to the last, thinking of his family and his people, and asking that his body be returned to them for proper burial. If he were victorious, he would do the same for Achilles. And so the epic ends not on a note of triumph but on one of shared sorrow—Achilles and Priam have lost whom they have most loved. And the fighting, rather than having run its course, will resume in twelve days to its inexorable end. It is these twin notes of the glory and the futility of war that re-sound throughout the epic which both celebrates and critiques the heroic code which actuates these heroes.

II. VIDEOTAPE SYNOPSIS

The readings for this lesson take us from the news of the death of Patroclus to the death of Hektor and, initially, to the return of Hektor's body to old Priam. In these last books of the Iliad, our interest is firmly centered on the two great heroes of the epic, Achilles and Hektor. Note how each represents a different conception of the hero.

III. VIDEOTAPE COMMENTARY

This discussion is focused around a number of questions which I put to the class.

1.   What is your view of human life as it is portrayed here? Do you see it as sad, pathetic and tragic, or do you see it as honorable and heroic?

Virginia sees it as heroic. The family was so important and people were willing to die for it. The state was even more important. Your performance was a part of a bigger something. Note here that Virginia is talking about the Trojans. I suggest that Achilles' extraordinary abilities set him apart from the crowd. Apart from his friend Patroclus, he is not seen surrounded by friends, children. His

Helen feels that there is both pathos and honor. There is so much destruction, so much ego-driven destruction but, at the end, higher values present themselves as well. I ask them who apart from Hector are the admirable characters? Helen says that for her Priam is. He kisses the hands of the man who murdered his son. He is forgiving rather than seeking revenge. He goes against what is almost what we consider human nature. He does the thing that is ennobling. Valeria agrees, saying that Achilles is revengeful, whereas Priam is forgiving. I remind the class that the foot soldier necessarily takes on the role of dehumanizing the enemy. The Iliad regularly presents situations in which enemies find commonality, which in fact is their humanity. In Book 24 we see glimpses of the possible, i.e. we are allowed to see that the relationship between the adversaries need not be what it actually is.

Barbara M. questions the use of the word "heroic." She sees it as a male, macho society, and there is very little mediation taking place. I agree, saying that this is the book that taught the males how to be the males. I assert myself; I leave a mark. A position of leadership commits you to a course of action, often to a course of action and its end. Gods do not exculpate individuals but gods represent the irrational force in human nature, the passion. Ada asserts that there is a certain amount of spiritual centering to be observed in the Iliad. The heroes listen to individual gods and heed their advice. This is an interesting point and brings up a discussion of the role of the gods on Greek society at the time Homer wrote the Iliad and at the time when the events in the Iliad took place, some four centuries earlier. I suggest that the relationship between heroes and gods was utilitarian. I'll do this if you do that. This was not an organized religion like, for instance the Hebrew religion, but rather these gods gradually assumed human traits and shape, in an evolutionary process which began with most gods being in fact animals. I suggest that for further reference students should read: Five Stages of Greek Religion by Gilbert Murray.

2.   You've shown that you liked the Trojans. Do any of you like any of the Greeks?

Agnes likes Patroclus. He was the soft side of Achilles. I try to get the class to understand the context of the time, by speculating on what avenues for immortality did they have in the face of death? Their immortality was through their sons. Sons will go out into the world, do something great, and you will be remembered. Hector's wish for his son is for him to kill his enemy, rip out their hearts, and eat them. That is a great deed. The imagery presented on Achilles' shield made for him by Hephaestus is a simile of normal life, juxtaposed with the reality of war. Susan adds that in that macho world as it was, men wept freely when they felt pain, physical or emotional. Achilles cried when Patroclus was killed; if he had not, no one would have understood it.

3.   Is this a pro war or anti war epic?

Phyllis thought that it shows the futility of battle. The futility of the scene is embedded in Achilles' shield. It's anti-war. I suggest that war brings out the best and the worst in human beings. The Iliad shows you those two extremes. Is there anything on the scale of values higher than life itself? Would you choose a long, boring life over a short and memorable one, marked by a great deed? The choice in Iliad is clearly the latter, there is something more important than life, as life itself is a thin thread.

Susan then brings up the interesting point that gang mentality in many ways is similar in its heroic code to that of the Iliad. The reasons for gang grouping, for seeking support, and for imposing the code of honor in the Iliad is not any different from all those things in modern day urban gangs. It is tribal. I suggest to the class that for an understanding of gang mentality as it relates to the ancient Greeks they should read Aeschylus' Oresteia.

Ada then brings up another modern connection, saying that other realms in the society, such as academia, are not free of war. Business is war by other means. Elaine adds that this young man's world and set of choices seems to be defined by the desire to make your mark in a flame of momentary glory, whereas older men may legitimately choose to make their mark in less spectacular ways, over longer time. I point to Nestor as the quintessential old man in the <u>Iliad</u>. He is wise, but also a little comical, pathetic. He's a real windbag. Rosemary puts a modern twist on the discussion by asserting that it is quite possible that choosing a longer route to honor is more difficult and therefore more honorable. I agree saying that modern literature says that living in a world that alienates you at every turn and strips your life of meaning is a heroic deed in itself. Eric defends Nestor, saying that the old guys are the memory of the tribe. Nestor survived to be old and they are counting on him to remember them. He is a storehouse of heroic memory.

4.   Is Achilles a tragic character?

Barbara M. feels that he is enamored with pride and honor, and therefore is tragic. Virginia says that his tragedy lies in his inability to change his destiny, although I point out that that would make us all tragic. Even his being empowered to do certain things was destiny, i.e. he had to do them whether he wanted to or not. That, alas, is the human condition. ♣

 *Now, please enjoy the videotape.*

IV. REVIEW QUESTIONS

1. In allowing Patroclus to enter the battle, is Achilles compromising the principles that he claims have actuated him? Does he sacrifice his best friend to his own selfish concerns?

2. Achilles' shield in Book XVIII presents a comprehensive view of human life in the heroic age. Do the scenes on it throw light on the meaning of war? Do they make the tragic pattern of the <u>Iliad</u> more stark?

3. Does Hektor's fear in the face of Achilles in Book XXII undermine his heroic stature? Is Achilles' savagery after his victory dishonorable behavior?

4. Is the encounter between Achilles and Hektor a symbolic one? Do they represent different principles?

5. In the meeting of Priam and Achilles in Book XXIV, which is the more tragic figure? If they are both tragic, is the source of their tragedy the same?

6. Is the <u>Iliad</u> propaganda for war? Protest against it? Neither? Both?

V. FURTHER READING

Bespaloff, Rachel. <u>On the Iliad</u>. New York: Pantheon Books, 1947

Denby, David, "Does Homer Have Legs?" <u>The New Yorker.</u> September 6, 1993

Murray, Gilbert. <u>Five Stages of Greek Religion</u>. New York: Doubleday Anchor Books, 1955

Steiner, George and Fagles, Robert, eds. <u>Homer: A Collection of Critical Essays</u>. Englewood Cliffs, NJ: Prentice Hall, 1962

NOTES

LESSON 5: SOPHOCLES, OEDIPUS THE KING

 Before you read this chapter of the Study Guide

READ: Text: Maynard Mack, Ed., Norton Anthology of World Masterpieces, vol. 1, pp. 652-701
Sophocles, Oedipus the King

I. INTRODUCTION

Oedipus the King has a special place in literature as, perhaps, the most important and most influential play ever written. It is certainly the world's most famous play and, since Aristotle, has attracted commentary after commentary from readers. One might begin one's study of the play by asking why the play is considered so important. Why has the play held the attention of every generation of readers? What does the play tell us about ourselves? What are its themes?

What strikes most moderns about the play is its extraordinary tragic intensity, which arises not so much from the horror of Oedipus' patricide and incest but from the sense of the blindness and helplessness of the human beings in the play, especially of the "greatest of all men," Oedipus. Ever the religious conservative, Sophocles wished to drive home a topical lesson for those contemporary religious skeptics who believed, like the sophist Protagoras, (note that on the videotape I refer to him mistakenly as Pythagoras) that "man is the measure of all things," a dictum which denies the existence of natural or divine justice in the world. He wished to show them, through the example of Oedipus, the utter insignificance of even a great man before the power of the gods.

Yet Sophocles is not a fatalist either. Despite the inexorable working out of fate, human beings are considered responsible for their acts. But to what extent are the human beings free and to what extent are they governed by necessity? In other words, if character is destiny to what extent is character fixed and unchangeable?

One thing stands certain in Sophocles' moral universe: "tuche," or chance, does not rule the world, despite what both Oedipus and Jocasta assert as they scoff at the validity of oracles. Such propositions serve to undermine the whole structure of religion and morality and to deny man's responsibility for his acts. If Jocasta and Oedipus were right, it would be a universe without purpose or plan, without order or harmony. In the end, the gods emerge triumphant, even if it is at the expense of humanity.

II. VIDEOTAPE SYNOPSIS

The discussion focuses on the nature of tragedy, the concept of "moira" (fate) vs. "tuche" (chance), Sophocles' religious conservatism and his speculation about human nature. What besides his own destruction does Oedipus gain? What does it mean to be human? How should one live? Does Oedipus suffer justly? Is the play a celebration of the tragic hero?

III. VIDEOTAPE COMMENTARY

I suggest you read this section before you watch the videotape. You will find that it will help you organize your thoughts in a more useful way than if you just watch the tape "cold." When you have finished viewing the tape you may want to read this section again.

I begin by saying that the shift from the Iliad to Oedipus the King is a shift from the tribal culture to the culture of the "polis," the Greek city-state. Virginia says that she found Oedipus much easier to read than the Iliad. This is a common observation. Oedipus is much more direct. Also, there is a difference between epic form and dramatic form. Epic form as used by Homer allows countless opportunities to build and release tension, with lots of peaks and valleys. With drama it is much more tersely wrought. It is a build and a release and that's it. It could be either the downfall or the celebration of the hero.

I then spend some time going over with the class a short synopsis of the story, including the prophecy Oedipus' father (Laius) receives - that Oedipus is without his knowledge going to kill his father and marry his mother. Consequently Oedipus is left on a mountain slope to die, but is found by a shepherd, and ends up with his adoptive parents in Corinth. Upon being called a bastard by an inebriated wedding guest, Oedipus consults the Oracle at Delphi on this subject, and the prophecy from the beginning of the story is confirmed. Unlike the epic, which would provide all the details of the past, in the drama we see one day in the life of Oedipus.

We then look at some of the conventions. There are some conventions that take you out of time and place. The most obvious example is the seer Teiresias, the blind man who is able to take you out of the present and into the future or the past. There is only one plot line. The unities of time, place and action are followed by Sophocles. Time: it all has to happen in the amount of time that it takes to see the play. Place: this whole play takes place in front of the gates of Thebes. Action: one plot.

I then ask the class if this is a tragedy of fate or is this a tragedy of character? I get no real answer for this from the class. Certainly, Oedipus's position as a king was made more insecure by the fact that he was Oedipus Tyrannous, meaning that he did not become king through natural succession. Jocasta does not believe that there is a coherent force ruling the universe, but rather that the universe is ruled by chance. Events, however, proved her quite wrong. The classic Sophoclean irony is that every step Oedipus takes to avoid the fate predicted by the oracle takes him closer to it. The oracle predicts the future, and Oedipus being the kind of man he is, fulfills the prophecy.

We now turn to Oedipus' flaw. Greek tragedy usually involves a good man, but not a perfect one, who through some flaw falls to ruin. I ask the class, what is Oedipus's flaw? Valeria sees it as something in him that makes him pay attention to the rumors. His virtues are his flaws.

Next we look at Oedipus' qualities. The suppliants know that he solved the riddle of the Sphinx, therefore he is intelligent. He is self assured, he is sympathetic, there is empathy, then he is pious, he sent Creon to the Oracle at Delphi to find out what to do. He is a man of feeling and sympathy which deepens his agony at the end of the play. If Oedipus, the best of men, who always made the right, rational decision, has to suffer through this, what happens to me? However, the tragedy of Oedipus, the suicide of his mother, the death of his father, his blindness are not exactly futile. The plague is gone, he saved the city and he is a hero.

The discussion now turns to the issue of guilt. Barbara M. holds that Oedipus is guiltless, he is not guilty of patricide and incest. I point out that Aristotle in The Nichomachaen Ethics says that for an act to possess moral consequence there must be consciousness of the will. Oedipus indeed does not know, therefore he is not guilty. Perhaps what Oedipus feels at the end of the play is not guilt but a great deal of shame for what he has done, i.e. committing the two great taboos, killing a parent and having sexual relations with a parent. Eric suggests that what else is gained is that he comes to self knowledge, finds out who he is. He makes a good point. What Oedipus wins is not simply the knowledge of his lineage, but he comes to see himself as a human being, he comes to know that to be human is to be blind. To be human is to be limited. Life is a hazard, it is groping. The answer to the question, who am I? is man, just as that is the answer to the Sphinx riddle (what walks on 4 legs in the morning, on two legs in the afternoon, and three legs in the evening?). He thinks he knows where his parents are and is not worried about the prophecy. His tragedy is in discovering that all the premises on which he built his life, all of them perfectly rational, were utterly false. The play is about the difference between appearance and reality. Man mistakes what seems to be for what is. Light imagery associates with knowledge. Sight imagery associates with knowledge. The play reverses the imagery, it is the blind man who sees, it is the darkness that provides knowledge. The fulfilling of the prophecy argues for the existence of divine will at work and against chance. Pythagoras, the skeptic, the rational thinker, said man is the measure of all things. Sophocles' play suggests something quite different. The gods' will is done, and the oracles have an inexorable quality of working themselves out. As Aeschylus puts it in his play, Prometheus Bound, "Science (in the sense of knowledge) is weaker than nature is." Chad surmises that his "hubris" is his reliance on his ability to make the right decision, and he found parallels with Genesis in this regard. Knowledge is a gift but it comes at a great cost. Oedipus sees more as a result of his struggle. ❧

 *Now, please enjoy the videotape.*

IV. REVIEW QUESTIONS

1. Does Oedipus have a tragic flaw which results in his downfall? Explain.

2. Review the speeches by the Chorus. What seem to be its principal functions in the play? What is its relationship to the action?

3. Comment on Oedipus' action in blinding himself. What is his motivation? What do other characters think of the blinding? Does his self-punishment modify your conception of his character?

4. Discuss the many references to "light," "sight," and "blight" in the play. Are they thematically related? Do they have any relationship to the view of human life expressed by the Chorus in its final speech?

5. The play is a masterpiece of dramatic irony (the tension between what the characters know and what the audience knows). Even Oedipus' name, "swollen-foot," is ironic, since we (but not the characters) know that it is evidence of the truth revealed at the end. What is the relation between this dramatic technique and the emphasis in the play upon the existential problems of knowing oneself and knowing what is "true" in the external world?

6. A "hero" might be defined not just as a good person, but as a person who embodies the value system of an entire culture. Could Oedipus be described as a "rationalist" hero?

V. FURTHER READING

Berkowitz, Luci and Brunner, Theodore F., trans. and ed. <u>Oedipus Tyrannus</u>. New York: W. W. Norton and co., 1970.

O'Brien, Michael J., ed. <u>Twentieth-Century Interpretations of Oedipus Rex</u>. Englewood Cliffs, N. J: Prentice Hall, 1968.

Seale, David. <u>Vision and Stagecraft in Sophocles</u>. Chicago: University of Chicago Press, 1982.

Winnington-Ingram, R. P. <u>Sophocles: An Interpretation</u>. Cambridge, Mass: Cambridge University Press, 1980.

NOTES

LESSON 6:   SOPHOCLES, ANTIGONE

  _____

Before you read this chapter of the Study Guide

READ: Text: Maynard Mack, Ed., Norton Anthology of World Masterpieces,
       vol. 1, pp. 701-739
       Sophocles, Antigone

I.   INTRODUCTION

I first read <u>Antigone</u> in the early '70's as a graduate student at the University of Maryland teaching a course in ancient and medieval world literature. For some reason, the play had simply fallen through one of the many ever-widening cracks in my reading (I'm sure you know the feeling). Those were heady times on college campuses. Student protests against the Vietnam War were met, in some cases, with riot police and tear gas. I can still remember the Maryland National Guard occupying our campus and my having to show identification to get into the building which housed the English Department.

<u>Antigone</u> was a favorite among my students because it so starkly spoke to our conflicts with the laws and powers of the state. Antigone's very moving soliloquy on individual freedom of conscience (p. 714) seemed to speak to our generation in a way that many of my students found remarkable for a piece of "classical" literature. Of course, we all read the play in very stark terms. Creon was President Nixon; Antigone was us. Creon was the villain; Antigone the hero. Creon was simply tyrannical; Antigone a martyr for a righteous cause.

Now that I am a little older and a bit better read, I find the play to be considerably more complex than I had once thought. Creon no longer strikes me as the cardboard heavy of melodrama. Indeed, as king he must uphold civil order and the gods of the state. Likewise, Antigone must uphold the family and the gods of religion. Since neither yields position, tragedy ensues.

My guess is that you, like the students on the teleclass, will side with Antigone in this conflict. But do consider Creon's position, especially in light of the Polynices-Eteocles battle. Faced with insurrection, it is no wonder that he wishes to make an object lesson of the fallen Polynices who has led a foreign force against his own city. And it is little wonder that order in the state should be among his highest values.

II.   VIDEOTAPE SYNOPSIS

The classroom discussion focuses on the question of whether a citizen's first duty is to the law of the state or to the law of religion. Other discussion points are: who is the tragic protagonist of the play? whose tragedy is it? are Creon and Antigone equally right and equally wrong or does Sophocles favor one over the other? does the play have contemporary applications?

Video interview with:

Justice Seymour Simon, Former Justice, Illinois State Supreme Court

III. VIDEOTAPE COMMENTARY

I suggest you read this section before you watch the videotape. You will find that it will help you organize your thoughts in a more useful way than if you just watch the tape "cold." When you have finished viewing the tape you may want to read this section again.

A. *Opening class discussion*

Antigone looks at the struggle between individual conscience and the law of the state, a very difficult issue that we in democracies wrestle with on an almost daily basis. It dramatizes the movement from the tribe to the city, to the "polis," where we have to get along with one another. Loyalty to the state is in conflict with either loyalty to religion or loyalty to our individual conscience.

Rosemary brings up the issue of conflict between Creon and Antigone as a man versus woman issue. The verbal struggle between men and women is present throughout the text. Creon will not be ruled by a woman. Antigone, however, exhibits a striking similarity to her father.

Barbara M. asks if the shame of Oedipus is wiped out after his death and is not carried on in Antigone. This is essentially true. In fact, I mention that Oedipus became so popular among the Athenians that poor old Sophocles had to write a play in which he was rewarded and made closer to the gods (Oedipus at Colonus).

Valeria mentions that Creon must have felt doubly betrayed by Antigone, because Antigone was a family member. And if he couldn't rule his family how could he rule the state? Indeed, Creon had a lot of problems with his family, especially with his son.

This brings the discussion to a consideration of whose side the audience might be on. I point out that the chorus is frequently used as a device to be the audience's representative on the stage, and it guides the audience's response to the action. The chorus in Antigone takes Antigone's side only very late in the play. There is a tendency in this play to see it as melodrama rather than tragedy. There is a tendency for moderns to see Antigone as right and Creon as wrong. Creon is the villain and Antigone is the hero. That falsifies the play. It is quite clear that the chorus sides with Creon through much of the play, and the original audience would probably do the same. At the beginning of the play Antigone is all alone. Slowly through the course of the play people start moving to her side. Creon finally does it but alas it's too late. The play is hard on the audience because we feel a strong pull toward Creon as well.

I then ask the "simple" question: Whose tragedy is it? Agnes thought it was Creon's tragedy. He loses his wife, his son, and sustains damage to his reputation although he remains the king at the end of the play. Barbara M. feels that Antigone is not blameless. She sees her as willful, citing the point at which Ismene wanted to join her but she said no, I want to do this all by myself, I want the fame, I want the power, and I want the honor.

I point out that Sophocles uses many techniques to distance the audience from Antigone: as Barbara M. points out, the way she treats her sister, her mentioning her betrothed only once in the entire play, the abstractness of the goals for which she strives, and her desire to be perceived as a martyr achieve this. This is not a melodrama (good guys and bad guys), because neither Creon nor Antigone is entirely right or wrong, although the play ultimately comes down on the side of the conservative religious view, and sides with Antigone.

Chad then makes a good point in Antigone's defense, saying that if she distances everyone who is close to her from herself, it will be easier for her to go through this difficult experience. It is something noble.

B. Interview with former Illinois State Supreme Court Justice Seymour Simon

I begin the interview by asking him whether he had sympathy with Creon in this play or does he feel that his policies simply are unjust?

Justice Simon felt that the government has a right to perpetuate itself and punish and to oppose rebellion and treason. On the other hand if Antigone felt strongly enough about the moral and religious need to have her brother buried, he could understand her motivations, but felt that she must suffer the consequences. However, he felt that the play represented a conflict of two rights, although Antigone thought that she was opposing a wrong, and that often there is a greater moral right in the objection than in the moral authority of the state.

I then asked him if we set the play in America today, wouldn't we find in favor of Creon rather than Antigone? Justice Simon saw Antigone's position not only as a religious one but as a moral one. However, if Creon had succumbed, that would have weakened his own authority and perhaps his own ability to survive. If Antigone had attracted enough people to her side, and if they threatened Creon with overthrow, he might have changed his mind. Antigone is alone, she is not a Rosa Parks; there was no ground swell of support for her.

Finally I asked whose tragedy it was. Justice Simon felt that it was Creon's tragedy. He is a very tragic figure. He was a lonely figure and not a hero by any standards. If there had been an election he would have lost it.

C. Final class discussion

Justice Simon speaks to the strong political undercurrent in this play. Usually in Greek plays which feature a heroine, the chorus is a chorus of women. Here the chorus is a chorus of old men, which further isolates them from Antigone. She needs to win them over to her point of view, and it doesn't happen until the very end when a sudden shift of sympathy takes place.

There was some discussion as to how much of a rebel Polynices really was, since he had a legal right to the throne. He was to share it with his brother, Eteocles, one year on and one year off. However, Eteocles did not give his throne up at the end of his rule, and Polynices went to seek help from the Argive army to invade Thebes. This was a big part of the problem, and of the political background of Antigone's action. Susan points out that although Antigone loves both her brothers equally, the potential of Polynices' triumphing with his foreign allies would bring disaster to Thebes, and that's why the sympathy for Creon is understandable.

I then relate this story with the Vietnam War issue in this country. The ethics, the group sentiment, was in a clash with the morality, which is higher than ethics. The state has power at its disposal which most of those advocating the moral choice don't have. The individual conscience, the morality point of view, is unable to win consensus and win over the ethos, but the struggle is always present. What makes Antigone so extraordinary is her willingness to go against the power of the state; people like that are rare.

Barbara M. points out that the Vietnam War opponents did win out at the end, after the struggle, which confirms that the outcome of the struggle is rarely easy to predict. Susan mentions the abortion issue, and says that she agrees with her daughter who says that the two poles represented have no fruitful dialogue, but are trying to shout each other down.

I mention that in the history of the civil rights struggle we see that the consensus often wins out. The modern analogies to this play are many. Ada offers the opinion that the bottom line is that the burden is on each individual to decide what is right and what is wrong, regardless of ethic or moral considerations in general. I respond that the didactic aspect of the play is shown by the fact that the audience reaches a consensus in its agreement with Antigone, and not the actors in the play. The consensus is reached in the audience, and not in the play. Barbara M. comments that we are trying to separate church and state. Recently a religious group took issue with the government regarding their right to sacrifice animals in their religious rites, and they won. Virginia suggests that Antigone's stand is made stronger with her knowledge that she would be stoned to death. Being shot by a firing squad is an altogether different thing from having your body broken in the most painful way. Susan and Rosemary both comment that Antigone suffered the fate of all prophets in the hands of the crowd, but by committing suicide, she deprived them of the opportunity to take her life, which in their view was the ultimate punishment, and in her view the ultimate sacrifice. I end the discussion by suggesting that Creon's luck is sad to be sure, but Antigone is the tragic hero here, as she is the one who opposed the force. Like Oedipus, Antigone is not crushed by her fate, but is ennobled by it. ♣

 *Now, please enjoy the videotape.*

IV. REVIEW QUESTIONS

1. From reading the opening dialogue between Ismene and Antigone, what inferences can you make about their relationship, about the character and values of each woman, and about the role of women in Thebes?

2. Does Antigone have a tragic flaw? What is it?

3. Does Creon have a tragic flaw? What is it?

4. Who is the play's protagonist?

5. Three innocent people in the play — Antigone, Haemon, and Euridyce — commit suicide. How and why do these suicides have a different moral coloring than Jocasta's suicide in Oedipus the King?

6. In what ways is Antigone like her father?

V. FURTHER READING

Aeshylus. Seven Against Thebes. New York: Oxford University Press, 1973

Goheen, Robert. The Imagery of Sophocles' Antigone. Princeton: University Press, 1951

Knox, Bernard. The Heroic Temper. Berkeley and Los Angeles: University of California Press, 1964

Seale, David. Vision and Stagecraft in Sophocles. Chicago: Chicago University Press, 1982

Segal, C. P. "Sophocles' Praise of Man and the Conflicts of the Antigone." In T. Woodard, ed. Sophocles: A Collection of Critical Essays. Englewood Cliffs, N. J: pp. 62-85, 1966

LESSON 7: VIRGIL, THE AENEID, BOOKS I, II

☞ *Before you read this chapter of the Study Guide*

READ: Text: Maynard Mack, Ed., Norton Anthology of World
Masterpieces, vol. 1, pp. 841-877

I. INTRODUCTION

I first read The Aeneid during my senior year at the Brooklyn Preparatory School (New York) —
fifty to seventy-five lines per night in the original Latin. I will not pretend that I enjoyed its literary
merits at the time. It wasn't so much that I couldn't see the forest for the trees; it was more like not
being able to see the tree because I was focused so intently on the twigs in the branches. As for the
forest, I didn't know there was one. Remembered through the mists of time, I recall a task both
daunting and humbling, but I remember it fondly nonetheless.

When I first taught The Aeneid, I learned that all that translating finally paid its dividend. I was
familiar with the text in a way that few of my colleagues were - the shadings of meaning, the subtle
intonations of language, the important concepts behind the poem (e.g. "pietas," "paterfamilias,"
"gravitas," "mos maiorum"). Perhaps this is the reason I chose to do three lessons on The Aeneid.
But I think there are more compelling reasons, besides the purely literary ones.

It seems to me that The Aeneid speaks to us as end-of-20th-century Americans in very familiar
terms. As we look back at our history as Americans, we now look at the enormous suffering of
innocent people that was part of the "cost" of the American nation — the slaughter of Native Americans, the exploitation of immigrants, the enslavement of blacks, to name but a few. No longer do we
look back through the innocent lens of an earlier Hollywood.

Virgil, too, sees the enormous cost in innocent lives necessary for the founding of Rome and its
civilization. And in his character of Aeneas, he creates a complex and sometimes tortured epic hero,
very different in kind from his Greek predecessors, Achilleus and Odysseus. As you read The
Aeneid, pay attention to Virgil's tone. "Sunt lachrymae rerum," literally translated as "these are the
tears of things," is the essential Virgilian tone. Be sure to listen for how Virgil celebrates the greatness of Rome even as he measures its price.

II. VIDEOTAPE SYNOPSIS

The discussion focuses on the distinctly Roman hero of Aeneas, Virgil's purpose in writing the epic,
the ambivalence of his epic vision as he celebrates Rome's greatness even as he measures its stagger-
ing cost, and his indebtedness to Homer. This class focuses on Book II (The Fall of Troy).

Video interview with:

Professor Maynard Mack, Yale University, Editor of The Norton Anthology of World Masterpieces

III. VIDEOTAPE COMMENTARY

A. *Initial classroom discussion*

The lesson begins with a short reading of the opening lines of <u>The Aeneid</u> in Latin by Professor Nuttall of Oxford. As you listen to it, try to focus on the cadences, the sound of the Latin. The discussion then begins with a short comparison between Homer and Virgil. One basic distinction is that Homer writes a folk epic, whereas Virgil writes an art epic. It is self consciously artistic. One of the initial questions from the class dealt with the fact that what Virgil wrote was not original, that he was re-telling an earlier tale. I explain to them that originality was not at the top of the artistic scale of values in the classical world, nor was it in the medieval or the renaissance world. That really is a modern idea. Virgil depends upon his audience knowing Homer. He is writing for a learned audience, for an upper class audience, which is extremely well educated. The notion of imitation is built into the fabric of classical literature and makes the experience of reading the literature richer.

We then set the context for the work. Virgil's dates are roughly 70 BC to 19 BC in Rome. It is Rome in one of its most powerful periods. Augustus is in power, and the "pax Romana" rules the Mediterranean and territories beyond. At the same time it is a period where the Romans are experiencing some of the uncertainties of expansionism. All sorts of strangers are flooding into Rome and are questioning things, strange customs are in town, and Rome is moved from a homogenous society into a multicultural society, with problems of diversity not unlike those we are experiencing in our society today. To the Romans of that time this was a real challenge. Virgil celebrates Rome's greatness, but he also undercuts it by suggesting the enormous price that must be paid for it on the individual and societal level. One of the impulses in the epic is political. The epic celebrates the hero, and the hero is the sum total of the values and virtues of that society. We will therefore start to define Aeneas as a hero.

We establish that Aeneas is very different from Achilles. The first words out of his mouth are "I wish I had died at Troy." Achilles would never say any such thing, it's unthinkable. Virgil's entreating Aeneas with telling the story is part of the epic writing technique, whereby the author sets the stage and then in a sense withdraws from it. Virgil reemerges on occasion to make comments, but he presents the story through Aeneas because it is much more powerful to do it that way than in the third person narrative. It gives an immediacy to the action. In the sense of guiding the emotional response, he is taking the place of chorus. Achilles is a free agent, but Aeneas carries burdens that Achilles does not carry. Barbara M. suggests that Aeneas was essentially a sensitive, feeling man, but his actions are limited in that he has to obey the dictates of the gods.

Eric asks how much evidence was there for Virgil's treating Rome as a Trojan colony. I reply that Virgil is dealing with history as his audience would understand it. The old oral legends held that Romans came out of the ashes of Troy. The defining epithet for Virgil was "pius," he was pious Aeneas. "Pious" essentially meant loyalty to the gods, the state, and to family. They are all tied together. The Romans think of the family as the state in miniature. As the state is ruled by the emperor, the family is ruled by the father. His authority was complete within the family. Also, it is loyalty to one's fellows. It is a dynamic concept, difficult to capture by a definition.

Next the discussion turns on the nature of the gods in the Aeneid. Jupiter, the more serene Roman equivalent of Zeus, is the force of order, and Juno is the force of destruction of others as well as self. Juno sends the storm to savage the Trojan fleet, and Jupiter calms it. Juno is the representative of the "furor impius," passionate, angry impiety. Virgil explains this seeming injustice by placing it in the hands of those forces in the universe that represent disorder and chaos. Aeneas is not allowed to rail against the gods. No Roman would applaud that kind of self indulgence.

B. Interview with Professor Maynard Mack

Professor Mack begins by commenting on the change in moving from the Homeric epic to the Virgilian epic. Virgil saw that the old kind of hero simply wouldn't do for the situation in his time which in not unlike the situation in our time. The old order had broken down, the old values had broken down, the old family values were broken down. There had been vast immigration from the east of people who were not ethnically the same as the Romans. There were insidious cults, like some of the ones we have in California, the old gods are gone too. In a situation like that a man is needed who is willing to give up all the things he would like to have had and work for the group. Aeneas was told that there are things more important in the world than your personal glory. The whole first part of the poem is an education in how to become a leader, a statesman, politician.

In the deeper human sense Aeneas shows us the commonality of human action, feeling, and concern. We all have to make choices and live with their consequences such as they may be. Although in our pursuit of our goals we are never given more than a glimmer of the goal, and are always partially in the dark regarding the appropriateness of our choice of goal and the way to achieve it.

C. Final class discussion

An important observation made is that in the first six books of the epic we watch the education of Aeneas. The first time we meet him he wishes he had died at Troy, because he thinks it would be heroic. That's the old code. He has to learn that the old code is dead. There are various levels of conflict to observe there. One of them is the cosmic conflict between fate (Jupiter) and counter fate (Juno). This is the struggle between reason and passion. Aeneas needs to learn to control his own passions. Just as the first scene in the epic is Jupiter calming Juno's storm, so is the first simile in Book One, the reasonable man calming the passions of the mob (where Juno represents the mob and Jupiter the reasonable man). The first six books of the Aeneid are the Odyssean portion of the epic and the last six books are the Iliadic portion of the epic. Reason will ultimately prevail, but Aeneas is the one who has to make it happen, at great personal cost.

In Book Six he makes a trip into the underworld, confronts his past, and at the end of the book is reborn, and prepared to face and fight the "impii," the impious ones. He meets Dido there, and comes out of the Sixth Book as pater Aeneas (the first time the epithet is used), his gaze now forward, no longer looking back. He is seemingly perfectly in control, although as you will see at the end of the epic when he confronts Turnus, this is not entirely true. As Professor Mack pointed out, Virgil probably had a didactic purpose in mind when writing this epic. He wanted to instruct his fellow Romans on the values needed at that time, but it can be read also for its pure narrative poetic value. Virgil being a sensitive man knew that this all came at great cost both for the individual and for the empire.

Barbara M. comments that Professor Mack mentioned choices, and that it seemed to her that Antigone and Aeneas made choices for the good of the group, whereas Agamemnon and Oedipus were more personally involved, making choices for their own gain.

The discussion then turns to that of the images in the work. As you will notice, the hunt imagery is everywhere. Dido is presented through a framing device, between two other characters, Penthesilea, Queen of the Amazons, the huntress, and Diana, the goddess of the hunt. Book Two is dominated by two images, both of destruction: fire and serpents. The verb used to depict the induction of the Trojan horse into the city was "insinuare," derived from the word, sinus, meaning the coils of the serpent. Notice also the hissing terminology depicting sleep coming over Agamemnon and Menelaus.

Similarly, when Aeneas gets to Carthage he is impressed with the activity and organization and likens Carthaginians to bees.

The first four books prepare us for the rest of the epic. They represent the movement from the old world of enmity toward the Greeks to the new world where he can befriend Greeks. ❧

Now, please enjoy the videotape.

IV. REVIEW QUESTIONS

1. Compare or contrast Achilleus with Aeneas as epic hero. Use the details of the epic to support and/or illustrate your assertions.

2. Discuss the dominant imagery of Book I and Book II. Are these patterns of imagery thematically important?

3. Discuss the role of the gods in Book II. How are Virgil's gods different from Homer's gods?

4. How is Aeneas' "pietas" demonstrated in Book II?

V. FURTHER READING

Bernard, John D., ed. <u>Vergil at 2000: Commemorative Essays on the Poet and His Influence</u>. New York: AMS Press, 1986

Camps, W. A. <u>An Introduction to Virgil's Aeneid</u>. London: Oxford University Press, 1969

Commager, Steele, ed. <u>Virgil: A Collection of Critical Essays</u>. Englewood Cliffs, NJ: Prentice Hall, 1966

Frazer, James. <u>The Golden Bough</u>. London: Macmillan, 1911

Griffin, Jasper. <u>Virgil</u>. Oxford: Oxford University Press, 1986

Knight, W. F. Jackson. <u>Roman Vergil</u>. 2nd. ed. Harmondsworth, UK: Penguin Press, 1966

Otis, Brooks. <u>Virgil: A Study in Civilized Poetry.</u> Oxford: Clarendon Press, 1964

Poschl, Viktor. <u>The Art of Vergil: Image and Symbol in theAeneid</u>. 1950, trans. Gerda Seligson, West Port, Conn: Greenwood Press, 1962

Williams, Gordon. <u>Technique and Ideas in the "Aeneid"</u> . New Haven, Conn: Yale University Press, 1983

LESSON 8:   VIRGIL, THE AENEID, BOOK IV

 Before you read this chapter of the Study Guide

READ: Text: Maynard Mack, Ed., Norton Anthology of World
Masterpieces, vol. 1, pp. 877-900

I.   INTRODUCTION

In terms of sheer human interest, no other Book of the Aeneid is quite as compelling as Book IV. Books I - III have narrated Aeneas' tragic history as epic survivor of the fall of Troy, destined to find a new civilization for his gods, his family and his people. The tableaux at the end of Book II of Aeneas carrying his father Anchises (the weight of Troy's past) on his back and leading his young son Ascanius (the future of Rome's promised greatness) by the hand as he flees the flames of Troy is given added poignancy as he loses his cherished wife Creusa in the ashes of Troy. Widowed, uncertain of his future, burdened with the awesome responsibilities of leadership, and exhausted by his storm-tossed wanderings in the Mediterranean it is natural that he should find in the extraordinary character of Dido and her remarkable achievements at Carthage a haven for himself and his followers. What Aeneas must learn in Book IV, however, are the awful limitations which the gods have placed on "pius" Aeneas.

II. VIDEOTAPE SYNOPSIS

This class concentrates on the tragedy of Dido.

Video interview with:
Professor A. D. Nuttall, New College, Oxford

III. VIDEOTAPE COMMENTARY

We suggest that you read this commentary before viewing the tapes. This preparation will help you make the most out of the class discussion.

A. Initial class discussion

This lesson deals with Book Four, probably the most famous book of the Aeneid. This is the stuff of operas and oratorios, and any number of operas can be mentioned dealing with Dido and Aeneas. I begin with asking the class, and I'll also ask you right now, "With whom do your sympathies lie, with Dido or with Aeneas?" Most of the class side with Dido. Is that your choice also?

Aeneas is often described as being "cold" at the end of the book. Dido finds love the second time over, and loses it again in what seems an abrupt and cold manner. She had other suitors whom she had rejected and then she herself is rejected. Similar to Oedipus, who as an earlier granter of favors finally turns into a beggar of favors, Dido grants favors to Aeneas in Book One and she is begging him at the end of Book Four.

Virginia's sympathy for Dido stems from the fact that Dido has been chosen by the gods to do this, and that we must really feel sympathy for her because she seems to have no choice. The gods manipulate her terribly. But Barbara C. sees Aeneas as manipulated also. He had to do what he had to do. He didn't want to do it but he knew that there was a bigger cause. This episode with Dido will become part of Aeneas' guilty past that he will try to undo in his trip to the underworld.

Some of the class comment on Aeneas' inability to express his feelings. Barbara M. feels that Aeneas represents the tongue-tied man who misunderstands himself, whereas Dido is a fully articulate woman capable of delivering her message in a passionate manner. Valeria suggests that Dido and Aeneas are the mortal representations of Juno and Jupiter. She is extreme in her passion, and he is almost an excess of reason, holding on to the qualities of "gravitas" and "pietas." Keeping emotions in check was what the Roman men were taught to do, which made them a relatively unemotional people. Therefore it was expected that if anyone were to indulge her passion and allow her city to go to ruin, it would be a woman. Notice also how the bee imagery in Book One is replaced by fire imagery in Book Four as it applies to the city of Carthage.

B. Interview with Professor A. D. Nuttall, New College, Oxford

Professor Nuttall begins the interview by likening Aeneas in Book Four to Shakespeare's Henry V, who is also cold and stilted, compared to Falstaff, because he is dedicated to the task of becoming a king. Virgil, who is famous for pity, pities his unlovable hero when he is trying to explain to Dido his reasons for leaving. Aeneas' quiet admission that he does not do what he does of his own will is in fact very moving.

He mentioned that the Aeneid reflects the Romans' tense awareness of their national destiny, that implicit in the story of Aeneas is the entire history of Rome. The Iliad by contrast was about individuals not nationalism.

Professor Nuttall maintains that there is all the way through the poem a sense of there being a terrible human price to pay for the epic imperial triumph. It is full of beautiful young people dying too soon.

Finally I ask him to comment on the tone of the work, on such stark phrases as "sunt lacrimae rerum" (literally: those are the tears of things) and "mens immota manet" (his mind remains unmoved). He reminds us that the next words are "lacrimae volvuntur inanes" (tears fall in vain), and suggests that the tears are not those of Dido, but of Aeneas. Aeneas wept, so that even within the triumphant epic hero you have this unappeased tragic feeling.

C. Final class discussion

Barbara M. says that she has trouble with Professor Nuttall's distinction between the Iliad and the Aeneid of one being a personal story and the other the story of a nation. In her view the poem is all about passion and poetry, and she saw the political aspects of it as merely the backdrop. I explain Professor Nuttall's view that in the Iliad there is always a sense of the present with occasional references to the past, whereas in the Aeneid there is a distinct sense of temporality, with a distinct timeline leading from the fall of Troy to the rise of Rome, and this is all a result of divine will, that Rome is a product of fate. Aeneas has to learn a certain passivity in the face of fate, which is what makes him different from the Iliadic heroes, who were all ego.

I then refer to the text and read the part in which Dido is consumed with flames of passion. Virginia says that her translation refers to the fire as a bog fire which means that it's not a real flame but that it's smoldering and the passion is under the surface. However, by the end of the book this slow fire has become a conflagration. Another quote from the book depicts Dido's emotional state of newly discovered love and in breaking her vow to her dead husband's body, she is preparing to give herself to Aeneas. The fire imagery in Book Four is very prominent as is the hunting imagery.

We then turn to Dido's suicide. Is it a confession of sin or is it dying for love? Barbara M. sees it as the result of her having nothing left - all her suitors were turned down, Aeneas has gone, she has been self-effaced, there was nothing left to do. Dido dies for love, Aeneas flees for duty. Eric states that there is another consideration that never comes up, which is that she would go with him. She can't do this, however, because she has her own duty, she is the Queen of Carthage. I suggest that her suicide is almost like an ironic self-punishment for what she has done, namely broken her vows to her husband "like a beast."

However, we do sympathize with Dido. But we must also see what limitations the gods place upon the hero, Aeneas. Dido follows her impulse even to her death, but Aeneas is a prisoner to a pattern, to a large cosmic force. What does he learn? Valeria suggests that he learns that there are forces above and beyond his control which he has to accept. Barbara M. gives a nice finishing touch to the discussion by remarking that this is the opposite of the usual tragedy of mind over heart, that this is a tragedy of heart over mind. I add that the conflict between head and heart becomes dominant in the western culture as we move through the Medieval period and through the Renaissance period. Reason places us close to the angels and passion places us close to the beast. As Hamlet says, "What a piece of work is man!" At the final bell, Barbara M. muses why love is always equated with madness. This is a good comment, but as I retort, Love is a divine madness! ♣

 *Now, please enjoy the videotape.*

IV. REVIEW QUESTIONS

1. Where do Virgil's sympathies lie in the Dido and Aeneas tragedy?

2. With whom do your sympathies lie? How has Virgil managed your sympathies?

3. What is the role of the gods, especially Juno and Venus, in the tragedy?

4. Analyze some of the patterns of imagery found in Book IV, especially those images which played such a central role in earlier Books — storm, fire, wounds, hunting.

5. What is Anna's role in Dido's tragedy? Does she help absolve Dido of guilt?

6. Victorian critics of the epic frequently commented on Dido's "guilt" in betraying her oaths to Sychaeus, her first husband. Do you see evidence of guilt in her betrayal of her oath or in her entering into what Victorian critics called a "pseudo-marriage" with Aeneas?

7. Analyze the simile of lines 585-596. What does the epic simile reveal about the character of Aeneas?

8. How do you view Dido's suicide - moral and noble? tragic? pathetic?

9. What effect does Virgil gain by having Aeneas say so very little in his own defense?

10. Similarly, what narrative effect does he gain by almost completely eliminating Aeneas from the last scenes of the Book?

11. At the very end of Book IV, Juno is described as "omnipotens" (l. 924). How thematically significant is this ironic epithet as applied to Juno?

12. If one theme of the first six books of the Aeneid is the education of Aeneas, what does Aeneas learn from the Dido tragedy?

V. FURTHER READING

Bernard, John D., ed. <u>Vergil at 2000: Commemorative Essays on the Poet and His Influence</u>. New York: AMS Press, 1986

Camps, W. A. <u>An Introduction to Virgil's Aeneid</u>. London: Oxford University Press, 1969

Commager, Steele, ed. <u>Virgil: A Collection of Critical Essays</u>. Englewood Cliffs, NJ: Prentice Hall, 1966

Frazer, James. <u>The Golden Bough</u>. London: Macmillan, 1911

Griffin, Jasper. <u>Virgil</u>. Oxford: Oxford University Press, 1986

Knight, W. F. Jackson. <u>Roman Vergil</u>. 2nd. ed. Harmondsworth, UK: Penguin Press, 1966

Otis, Brooks. <u>Virgil: A Study in Civilized Poetry.</u> Oxford: Clarendon Press, 1964

Poschl, Viktor. <u>The Art of Vergil: Image and Symbol in the Aeneid</u>. 1950, trans. Gerda Seligson, West Port, Conn: Greenwood Press, 1962

Williams, Gordon. <u>Technique and Ideas in the "Aeneid"</u>. New Haven, Conn: Yale University Press, 1983

LESSON 9: VIRGIL, THE AENEID, BOOKS VI, VIII, XI

☞ **Before you read this chapter of the Study Guide**

READ: Text: Maynard Mack, Ed., Norton Anthology of World
Masterpieces, vol. 1, pp. 900-917

I. INTRODUCTION

In terms of the education of Aeneas, Book VI is absolutely crucial. I encourage you to read it carefully, paying attention to how Virgil dramatically portrays the "death" of the Trojan Aeneas (as he confronts his guilty past) and his "rebirth" as the Roman Aeneas (achieved after his vision of the future greatness of Rome)—culminating in Anchises' reference to him as "Romanus." From this point on in the epic, Aeneas no longer yearns for the unretrievable world of Troy; his gaze is firmly fixed on the future promise of Rome. In short, his "pietas" has been redirected, his task is to fulfill Anchises' vision.

Books VII-XII, the Iliadic portion of the epic, depict the triumph of "pietas" over the forces of the "furor impii"—embodied in Mezentius and, most especially, in Turnus. Pay careful attention to Virgil's attitude toward war in these final Books. War is both a monster of destruction and a necessary evil leading ultimately to a greater good. A careful reading of Aeneas' shield in Book VIII reveals Aeneas' historical position. He is the link between Hercules in the distant past and Augustus in the distant future, who will establish the "pax Romana"—an orderly, creative and stable peace for Rome.

In the final scene of the epic, we see clearly the ambivalence of Virgil's vision as an angry Aeneas finally slays Turnus. Aeneas hesitates; he feels some sympathy for the fallen Turnus. His victory, if that is what we can call it, is for Rome not for himself. In this last struggle, Aeneas can only be the loser. His enslavement to his destiny has almost dehumanized him. From one point of view, he is more tragic than Dido. And on that last tragic note Virgil ends his epic.

II. VIDEOTAPE SYNOPSIS

This class focuses on Book VI (The Symbolic Death and Resurrection of the Hero).

Video interview with:

Professor A. D. Nuttall, New College, Oxford

III. VIDEOTAPE COMMENTARY

I suggest you read this section before you watch the videotape. You will find that it will help you organize your thoughts in a more useful way than if you just watch the tape "cold." When you have finished viewing the tape you may want to read this section again.

A. Initial class discussion

Barbara M. opens the discussion by asking where Aeneas is in this book. He is in the land of the dead, but is he also in hell? This is a good question. Although there is a section for punishment in

Virgil's underworld, it is not like Dante's inferno. This is the first lengthy description of the realm of the underworld that we have in Western Literature. There is a section of reward as well, Elysium, where Aeneas finds his father. There is also a section, described in the beginning as the mythological Hades, which is a realm of neither reward nor punishment.

Outline of Book VI

I.   Preparation (1-263)
    A. the landing (1-13)
    B. the temple doors (14-41)
    C. the prophecy (42-97)
    D. the conditions to be met (98-155)
    E. the conditions fulfilled (156-263)

II.   The Descent (The Mythological Hades) (264-547)
    A. the Vestibulum (Entrance) (264-294)
    B. the hither side of the Styx (295-383)
        1.   the "insepulti" (2945-336)
        2.   Palinurus (337-383)
    C. Crossing the Styx (384-416)
    D. Between the Styx and the Fork in the Road (417-547)
        1.   preliminary view
        2.   Dido
        3.   Deiphobus

III. The Left-Hand Road: Description of Tartarus (548-627)

IV.   The Right-Hand Road: To Elysium (628-678)
    A. the Fortress of Dis: Deposition of the Golden Bough (628-636)
    B. Elysium (637-678)

V.   The Philosophical Hades: The Valley Of Lethe And The Souls Of Future Romans (679-892)
    A. the meeting of Aeneas and Anchises (679 -702)
    B. the theory of Reincarnation (703-751)
    C. the Show of the Heroes (752-892)

VI.   The Reascent: The Two Gates (893-901)

I ask the class why the lovers are down there. Peter suggests that Dido was there because she broke her marriage vow to her husband, she committed suicide, and perhaps because she was in love. Indeed, almost everybody down there has violated the concept of "pietas" and has an excess of "furor." They have too much passion, their passion rules their reason and in doing so, they became something less than human. Note how Virgil in the end is kind to Dido, because after all she is returned to Sychaeus. Similarly note how touching is the scene in which Dido and Aeneas meet. It is the reverse of the scene in which they had parted. He says a lot in an attempt to explain his actions to her, and she hardly responds. The strong moral coloring of everything in this epic is very different from the Homeric epic.

Virgil's sense of destiny is strikingly opposed to Homer's permanent present, and his heroes desire to be remembered as heroes. The mythic journey undertaken in Book VI is the journey that almost every cultural hero ultimately undertakes, namely the death and resurrection of the hero. "Arma virumque cano" are the opening words of the epic. Book VI is the middle of the epic, between the two fields of action posited by the first words. The wanderings of the men are over, and the war in Italy has not started yet. A question is posed at the beginning of Book VI: Is Aeneas worthy of bearing the title "pater Aeneas?" The answer at the beginning of Book VI is "no," but at the end of Book VI it's "yes." It speaks to the death of the Trojan hero and the resurrection of the Roman hero.

For the first five books Aeneas was Trojan, and at the end of Book VI his father, Anchises, addresses him with: "Yours, my Roman, is the gift of government." The epithet "Romanus" is used here for the first time.

What happens in Book VI is what in modern terminology can be called facing the dark night of the soul. This is a situation when, confronting the self, we emerge from that confrontation regenerated through some philosophical principle upon which we set our life on a new axis. It involves a constant struggle between disorder and order, "furor impius" and "pietas," passion and reason.

As Aeneas descends into the underworld he encounters his past in reverse, Palinurus, the helmsman on his ship, who died after Dido, appears first, and is followed by Dido, then he meets Deiphobus, Helen's husband in Troy. Aeneas is going back over his guilty past, and in doing so he becomes purged of the past. The symbolic significance of the golden bough and its similarity to the mistletoe was addressed. It is a talisman which enables Aeneas to descend into the underworld and, more importantly, reemerge from it. The imagery of the golden bough is one of life in death.

B. Interview with Professor A. D. Nuttall , New College, Oxford

The interview begins with a discussion of Virgil's motives for writing the Aeneid. Virgil would say that what he wanted to do was to rewrite the Iliad and Odyssey into one big epic for his Roman people. What actually happens according to Professor Nuttall is that he turns the entire thing inside out, developing a completely different sort of values, and a new sort of poem. This involved inventing the notion of responsibility, something quite new to epics. Odysseus, for example, was not "responsible" for his actions. "Pietas" in its many meanings, some of which cannot be translated, includes as a crucial part the notion of responsibility to your family, to your fellow citizens, to tradition, etc. Aeneas is in that sense like a grown up man, and Achilles is a headstrong boy. Turnus, Aeneas' enemy in the epic, is the representative of "furor" which would have been considered a virtue by the Greeks. Aeneas' "pietas" is a concept opposed to "furor." This, in fact, says Professor Nuttall, represented a slight technical problem for Virgil, for he had to make it possible for "pietas" to defeat "furor" in war. He solved it by allowing the two concepts to coincide for a moment in what we can term a justified "furor," when Aeneas sees the belt of Pallas and thus can strike in righteous anger.

The recurring image of the slaying of the deer in the Aeneid indicates to Professor Nuttall that Virgil's sensibility was essentially pastoral. That act in this genre would be considered a terrible thing to do. This fact creates a sort of a conflict, as the historical direction of the epic was driven by events of a political nature quite at odds with the pastoral view of the world. Aeneas' marking of the ground when he first arrives on Latin soil is an example of what a good Virgilian would see as aggressive behavior against the pristine greenness of the pastoral. If the great justification of Rome is to bring law and order to the people, it is odd to see Rome bring those things to a people who don't actually require it. The Latin people were a people who are just by natural impulse, they are righteous spontaneously, because they are the pastoral Arcadian kind of people.

C. Final class discussion

The discussion follows up on Professor Nuttall's thesis that Virgil has a nostalgic sympathy for a simpler, pastoral world, a world which was destroyed by the creation of the empire. The forces of history have run over it rough shod. There is a remarkably striking similarity here to the modern world. Barbara M. adds that there is an acknowledgment of the necessity to be cruel to the enemy to the extent of having to kill him. The qualities of character that are necessary in the context of war are not always admirable when isolated. Pax Romana was primarily the consequence of having to be rational, which sometimes means being brutal, cruel, and dominating. Helen said that the values of "pietas," "gravitas" and self sacrifice were truly important, because, in future generations, those who were self indulgent were responsible for bringing down these empires.

Final comments dealt with the nature of Virgil's work. His epic is both a history and a book of instruction, it has a didactic value and purpose. The significance of Aeneas' leaving the underworld through the gate of the false dreams (instead of the gate of true dreams) was discussed, and I related that Professor Nuttall told me in another part of our conversation that he suspects that Virgil would have revised that part. Alternatively it may have been simply a device to inform the reader of the time-frame, as in folk lore false dreams occurred before midnight.

At the close of class we refer to the end of the book, where Aeneas stands over the fallen Turnus. Even here Virgil does not allow us to see the triumph without the cost. Turnus is presented as a perfectly sympathetic figure, and Aeneas' sword is frozen in the air for a moment by the conflict between "pietas" and "furor," and brought down with doubt lingering in the air. This epic is cut to life as we know it: it does not give us simple answers. ♪

 *Now, please enjoy the videotape.*

IV. REVIEW QUESTIONS

1. Compare Homer's description of the shield of Achilles in the Iliad to Virgil's description of the shield of Aeneas. Does each serve a similar function in the epic?

2. Compare Aeneas' reception in the underworld by Dido and by Anchises. Why does Virgil have Aeneas meet Dido in the underworld? What does Aeneas learn from each encounter?

3. Describe Virgil's attitude toward war in the last Books of the Aeneid. Why does he emphasize the effects of war on the survivors?

4. Characterize the tone of the last books of the epic.

5. Aeneas demonstrates pitilessness, cruelty, and righteous indignation among other qualities of character in the last Books. Are these desirable qualities in a leader?

V. FURTHER READING

Bernard, John D., ed. Vergil at 2000: Commemorative Essays on the Poet and His Influence. New York: AMS Press, 1986

Camps, W. A. An Introduction to Virgil's Aeneid. London: Oxford University Press, 1969

Commager, Steele, ed. Virgil: A Collection of Critical Essays. Englewood Cliffs, NJ: Prentice Hall, 1966

Frazer, James. The Golden Bough. London: Macmillan, 1911

Griffin, Jasper. Virgil. Oxford: Oxford University Press, 1986

Knight, W. F. Jackson. Roman Vergil. 2nd. ed. Harmondsworth, UK: Penguin Press, 1966

Otis, Brooks. Virgil: A Study in Civilized Poetry. Oxford: Clarendon Press, 1964

Poschl, Viktor. The Art of Vergil: Image and Symbol in theAeneid. 1950, trans. Gerda Seligson, West Port, Conn: Greenwood Press, 1962

Williams, Gordon. Technique and Ideas in the "Aeneid". New Haven, Conn: Yale University Press, 1983

LESSON 10:   DANTE, THE INFERNO, PART 1

 Before you read this chapter of the Study Guide

READ: Text: Maynard Mack, Ed., Norton Anthology of World
Masterpieces, vol. 1, pp. 1284-1467

I.   INTRODUCTION

Although it's heresy to say it, I never cease to be amazed at the enthusiasm with which students read The Inferno. And our teleclass students are no exception. Every time I teach it, I think that you will be turned off by the "medieval-ness" of Dante and every time you prove me wrong. Dante's vibrant and extraordinary tale of a journey both literal, autobiographical, allegorical, political and moral transcends its time, place and ideology and so speaks to us today just as it did to its original audience. Indeed, this may prove to be a good entry for you into the work: think about what is timeless about The Inferno.

I'd suggest paying attention to several things as you read The Inferno. First, notice how Dante uses the two traditions, classical and Judeo-Christian, in his epic. Second, try to read his poem as a medieval Catholic might to understand and "feel" the urgency and absolute quality of his message. Third, see Dante's descent as a symbolic one, each step taking him farther from God, each circle containing sinners whose sin (and, therefore, whose punishment) is more serious than the last. To understand why this is so, see the schema of the soul according to St. Thomas Aquinas. (This is outlined for you at the end of this section.) And last, pay careful attention to Dante the pilgrim's emotional response to the sinners, especially how he must learn to harden his heart during his journey. Do you share Dante's emotional response? Do you feel sympathy, for example, for Paolo and Francesca? Would you feel sympathy for those whose only "sin" was their homosexuality?

A Schema of the Powers of the Soul According to St. Thomas Aquinas

I.   The Concupiscible: this is the vegetative level which people share with all living creatures (i.e., plants and animals).

   a.) the generative power: concerned with reproduction and the preservation of the race. (CIRCLE 2)

   b.) the nutritive power: concerned with food and the preservation of the individual. (CIRCLE 3)

   c.) the augmentative power: desires individual growth and expansion. (CIRCLE 4)

II. The Irascible: the sensitive level which people possess as an animal whose knowledge comes through the senses.

   a.) the irascible passive: suffers the frustration of not satisfying the concupiscible powers.

     1.) may result in anger at not achieving earthly good (CIRCLE 5)

     2.) may result in anger at not achieving heavenly good (CIRCLE 6)

b.) the irascible active: reacts against the frustration and lashes out in anger and violence at others (CIRCLE 7)

III. The Rational or Intellectual: by which people are distinguished from material creation and through which they participate in higher creation, i.e., perceive God.

    a.) the intellectual passive: envy that plots the ruin of others (CIRCLE 8)

    b.) the intellectual active: pride with its excessive desire for glory and willful defiance of others (CIRCLE 9)

II. VIDEOTAPE SYNOPSIS

The discussion in this lesson centers on the nature of allegory, the law of symbolic retribution, and the structure of Dante's Hell as it reflects the Thomistic nature of the soul. How should one read <u>Inferno</u> for the first time? To what extent is Dante a new epic hero and his journey a new epic "action?" What is <u>Inferno</u> about? What is Dante's purpose in writing it? The episode of Paolo and Francesca is singled out for particular attention.

Video interview with:
Professor Zygmunt Baranski, University of Reading, England

III. VIDEOTAPE COMMENTARY

I suggest you read this section before you watch the videotape. You will find that it will help you organize your thoughts in a more useful way than if you just watch the tape "cold." When you have finished viewing the tape you may want to read this section again.

A. *Initial class discussion*

The thirteen hundred years intervening between Virgil's <u>Aeneid</u> and Dante's <u>Inferno</u> is a period during which the advent of Christianity entirely changed civilization in almost every aspect. Dante acknowledged Virgil as the master and himself as the student, but he did not suffer from false humility. He was one of the most prominent political and intellectual figures of his time, and definitely the best poet. The journey that he undertakes is not unlike the one undertaken by Aeneas in that it is a vicarious descent into his own conscience. Valeria points out that it is perhaps no accident that the journey starts on Good Friday. The three day journey of Jesus is replicated here by humans, making the religious experience of Christianity closer to life. It relates to our facing all of our sins, which are in all of us (at least as potential sins), regardless of our acting upon them or not.

The discussion next turns to the medieval Italian view of women, which was very complex. Dante was separated from his wife and children; he lived in exile for twenty years. He was a man of passion and talent and can not be assumed to have lived all this time in utter loneliness. Thus he understands Paolo and Francesca very well. Beatrice comes to represent heavenly love. She is one of the images of woman people held at that time, the idealized, divine object before which man bows.

Dante in his journey through the underworld is going through a learning process, just as Aeneas was put through one. One of the important things to watch is Dante, the pilgrim's, emotional response to what he sees the sinners go through, for instance with Paolo and Francesca. Paolo and Francesca's sin was adultery. Francesca was married to Paolo's brother, who was old and physically deformed. Paolo and Francesca's punishment in hell is that they are spirits unable for eternity to be completely united. Dante's emotional reaction is one of sympathy, he swoons in response to God's punishment of sin. However, the farther along he goes through the underworld, the less sympathetic he gets, until he gets downright abusive to the sinners. He hardens his heart as he moves downward through the circles.

B. Interview with Professor Zygmunt Baranski, University of Reading, England

Professor Baranski discusses the women in Dante. Beatrice he sees as essentially based upon a literary construct, upon an idealization of woman, which is very much a part of the romance vernacular tradition. What makes Dante's treatment of Beatrice new is that through the figure of Beatrice he brings secular and religious ideas of love together. In Divina Comedia Beatrice is the word of God, divinely illuminated, divinely inspired knowledge, that part of the divinity which continues to exist in the world, and helps it to achieve its salvation in a variety of ways.

Francesca and Beatrice are each other's antithesis. Both of them are involved with love, but Francesca sins because of love and Beatrice saves because of love. Francesca is from a psychological point of view a much more complex character than Beatrice is.

What Dante does according to Professor Baranski in that canto is instruct us on some ideological points. First, we can't ever quite understand God's justice; and secondly, no matter how insignificant the sins may seem to us, if the sinners are unrepentant they will go to hell. Francesca and Paolo never admit guilt. Francesca blames her predicament on "extenuating circumstances," which from the point of view of divine justice are really irrelevant. What matters are the marriage vows, and the fact that they were broken. This work encompasses a major discussion about sin, about personal attitude toward sin, and about responsibility.

C. Final class discussion

I begin this section by asking Chad the leading question, what is this old Italian epic about? Chad's response is that "it's about this guy called Dante who got stiffed by his contemporaries, and decided to get back at them by writing a little story." And on one level he is right. Agnes suggests that it's about the sins of the church, about the granting of benedictions for money, and general licentiousness. Peter offers the view that Dante means to show that not all sins are equal, that this is Dante's explanation of hell for the mortals, "a practical guide to hell."

I then talk briefly about the Ptolemaic cosmology which puts the earth in the ninth circle away from God, and Satan in the center of the earth. Dante places Satan in his ninth circle of hell, at the farthest distance from God. God is light and warmth. Satan is dark and cold. The sins get more offensive as you move further down through the circles of hell. The medieval metaphor of the "great chain of being" postulates orders of creation: one starts with God, and below God are the angels, then people, animals, plants, minerals and so on. We should aspire to move upward, but we are pulled down by what is below us. The sins of the intellect are punished most severely, and the carnal sins are dealt with more lightly.

A discussion followed of what one has to be to follow this story. Do you have to be a medieval catholic, a poet, or a modern psychoanalyst to understand it? My answer is, you have to be any or all of the above.

We then turn to the allegorical dark wood. Neither grace nor reason alone is sufficient to rescue one from them. It is Virgil and Beatrice that rescue Dante. Ada makes an important point: she asserts that belief and mental commitment to an idea are not sufficient for salvation, that you must perform actual deeds in real life which will ultimately lead to salvation. On one level we can read Dante as a modern discovery of the redeeming qualities of love, how one should live. The message transcends sects, religions.

Notice how the move from classical epic to medieval Christian epic is bringing a different kind of hero. This brings up a discussion of how easy or hard Dante was to read. How did you find it? One of the problems is that Dante's works are full of allegory and allegory is hard to read. Professor Baranski suggests that the best way to read The Inferno for the first time is to read it as an adventure story, not on a moral or allegorical level. It makes so many appeals to your senses that this approach is easily justified. This is the great masterpiece of the middle ages as it summarizes the middle ages. It also provides an inkling of what follows in the Renaissance, which is a celebration of humanism. Two traditions come together in the middle ages that appear to be incompatible: the Classical World (Greek and Roman writers), and the Judeo Christian tradition. The Inferno is a seamless combination of these two traditions. Barbara M. remarks that placing adultery in the second circle may have been convenient for Dante, but it remains one of the great sins, and she didn't particularly appreciate his ordering them in this way. However, I point out that this is not Dante's personal hierarchy of sins, but was the medieval way of assessing sin, which is certainly different from the modern one.

The discussion ends in answering Charles's question about how The Inferno was received in Dante's time. It was in fact received very well by the people, although not necessarily so by the church. Within fifty years of his death Dante was enormously famous, and Boccaccio was delivering lectures on him. His work was intelligible in that time at that place within the given adopted framework. Today, however, we have a more complex accumulation of ethics and morality that have arrived at a very sophisticated level, which makes this a more difficult time to read Dante in. We will continue this discussion in the next lesson. ✣

 *Now, please enjoy the videotape.*

IV. REVIEW QUESTIONS

1. Compare Dante to Achilleus and Aeneas. How is Dante a new epic hero?

2. Discuss how the penalty fits the sin in any three circles of your choice.

3. Discuss the role of Virgil. What does he represent? What are his limitations as guide?

4. Why is the Paolo and Francesca episode so short? What information is missing from the account? Does it matter to you that Francesca's marriage was not a happy one?

V. FURTHER READING

Auerbach, Eric. Dante, Poet of the Secular World. trans. Ralph Manheim, 1961.

Bernardo, Ado S. and Pellegrini, Anthony L. A Critical Study Guide to Dante's "Divine Comedy." 1968.

Clements, R.J., ed. American Critical Essays on Dante. 1969.

Freccero, J. Dante: A Collection of Critical Essays. Englewood Cliffs, NJ: Prentice-Hall, 1965.

LESSON 11:   DANTE, THE INFERNO, PART 2

   Before you read this chapter of the Study Guide

READ: Text: Maynard Mack, Ed., Norton Anthology of World
　　　　　Masterpieces, vol. 1, pp. 1284-1467

I.   INTRODUCTION

The energy and enthusiasm for Dante generated by the class members continues in the second hour of discussion. One wonders if Dante does not satisfy some need by modern readers for moral certainty and clear behavior parameters. Whatever the reason, The Inferno strikes a strong emotional chord among these experienced and thoughtful adults.

II.   VIDEOTAPE SYNOPSIS

A continuation of our discussion of Dante, Lesson 11 focuses on several different issues: its critical reception through the ages, its various levels of meanings, the nature of sin, and how we would rewrite the epic for today, which is to say, what sins we would throw out (gluttony?) and what sins we would add (any thoughts?).

III.   VIDEOTAPE COMMENTARY

I suggest you read this section before you watch the videotape. You will find that it will help you organize your thoughts in a more useful way than if you just watch the tape "cold." When you have finished viewing the tape you may want to read this section again.

A. *Initial class discussion*

The opening discussion touches on the personal animosity Dante feels towards his enemies and how he seems to use The Inferno to vent his anger and contempt for them. Virginia wonders whether there is more than allegory in his work. I point out that this is definitely true, and that part of the power of The Inferno is that it can be read on many different levels - allegorical, literal, moral, anagogical (that is, pertaining to searching for hidden, spiritual meaning, as in the Scriptures), and even biographical levels.   In terms of the biographical nature of the work, his personal attitude toward his enemies became, if anything, more intensely hateful after years of exile, and this is quite evident in his writing.

The discussion then turns to the classifications of the sins. As I point out, this was not Dante's personal line-up, he was simply following the traditional system of beliefs about the perceived severity of sins.

We note how the basic principle of organization, whereby the lighter sins, those stemming from material aspects of human existence are in the higher circles of hell, while those sins pertaining to the spiritual life are perceived as being more grave and are relegated to the inner circles, where the punishment is harsher. Francesca and Paolo's sin, for example, consists less of offending the moral code, less in lust, than in their relaxing their exercise of reason. They never confessed their sin. Others, however, are quite different. They seem to feel a compulsion to confess. It suggests that even the most fallen among us have something inside that seeks confession and punishment. From the modern point of view, transgressors get what they want, because, as Dostoyevsky was to say later, in committing a crime, the criminal in a sense also seeks punishment for that crime.

The next issue touched on was Dante's popularity through the ages. Immensely popular among his contemporaries and extolled by Petrarch and Boccaccio, Dante's star was very high until the early Renaissance, and then his popularity plummeted in the 17th and 18th centuries. Voltaire, for instance, found Dante just barbarous, and hated him. Dante was made popular again by Coleridge and other Romantics in the 19th century and remained so throughout that time. In the 20th century T. S. Eliot wrote a series of essays on Dante and in the 1960's there was an explosion of his popularity which has gone on essentially unabated to this day. We are all, like Dante, lost in the dark wood. He speaks to our age.

Virginia next makes the distinction between Virgil and Homer (where the gods play a large part in determining people's actions), and Dante, and that what becomes essential is the notion of individual responsibility for one's actions. Susan compares Dante to Christ, in that he is quite forgiving of people's weaknesses. Susan points out that the list of sins arranged in The Inferno from the slightest to the most severe would almost be reversed in our modern society. This led to a fascinating discussion on the nature of sin.

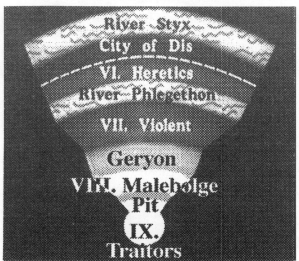

What sins from that list would we throw out these days? Valeria would take the lovers out of hell, and she noted that Dante is very sympathetic to Francesca and Paolo, swooning when he sees them. The class were quite unanimous about throwing out gluttony. After all, gluttons hurt themselves only, not others, so they are not too bad. Dante, as I point out, would not agree. For gluttons give in to passion, the passion of appetite. We then turn to the issue of suicide, which was not seen by many as a sin. But according to Dante, those who commit suicide are committing the crime of defiling the image of God. The social taboo against suicide remains strong to this day. We then turn to opportunists in business, Dante's usurers, those who make money from money, who were punished in Dante's hell and were deep on Dante's list, but we treat such people almost as heroes today. Heretics, those who in Dante's Inferno didn't believe in an afterlife, become problematic today, as we no longer question other people's beliefs in the way we used to.

Those placed in the 8th circle of hell, the "malebolge," are those whose sins hurt others. Today's politicians often seem to belong in this category, but we are more inclined to understand their position than Dante seemed to be. Dante's universe is a well ordered Ptolemaic universe, quite different from ours. Centuries later, the Copernican universe displaced Dante's universe forever. The notions of sin and virtue, good and evil, punishment and reward are much more complex today than they were in the organized universe in which Dante and his contemporaries lived. We end up asking are we rational animals, as the Greeks would argue or are we more animal than rational? Who is in the dark wood? Dante's pilgrim undertakes a painful journey. He knows that no one wants to die with sin and sin must be properly dealt with while we are alive, otherwise it's too late. ♣

VIII. MALEBOLGE

Seducers
Flatterers
Simoniacs
Fortune Tellers
Grafters
Hypocrites
Thieves
False Counsellors
Sowers of Discord
Falsifiers

 *Now, please enjoy the videotape.*

IV. REVIEW QUESTIONS

1. What do you make of the concept of Limbo for the virtuous pagans? Is that just?

2. Choose some notorious people from today's headlines or from history and place them in Dante's hell. Explain your reasons for placing them where you do.

3. In a canto of your choosing, analyze Dante's use of images. Are they thematically significant?

V. FURTHER READING

Please refer to the readings listed at the end of Lesson 10.

NOTES

LESSON 12:   SHAKESPEARE, HAMLET, PART 1

 Before you read this chapter of the Study Guide

R EAD: Text: Maynard Mack, Ed., Norton Anthology of World
Masterpieces, vol. 1, pp. 2014-2110

I.   INTRODUCTION

C oming to <u>Hamlet</u> for the first time can be an awfully daunting experience. You've probably heard of it as the greatest play in the English language, you've probably heard lines of it quoted throughout your life, and you've also probably heard that it is the most written about play in Western culture. The natural tendency, then, for beginning students is either to treat the play as some great cultural icon and bow in dutiful obeisance or to throw up your hands and chant, "I am not worthy." It is easy, in short, to forget that this is a play—designed for performance by actors before a live audience. I encourage anything you can do to make the text come alive for you—read it aloud, read along with a recording of the play, see a film version to supplement your reading (but remember films are not plays), or better yet, see the play in performance. It is in live performance that the text of <u>Hamlet</u> reveals its greatness.

<u>Hamlet</u> can be read in so many different ways and on so many different levels—Eliot called it the "Mona Lisa of literature"—that no introduction to it can do the play justice. In this first lesson, I ask you to consider the political implications of the play. Hamlet must act in a world of "seeming," where outward appearances frequently mask a very different "being." How does one act in such a world without adopting the methods and the values of that world? What are the necessary qualities of leadership in such a world? Is it necessary that a good king be a good person? Why?

II.   VIDEOTAPE SYNOPSIS

The discussion centers on Hamlet's unique prestige in Western culture as "THE" play, the Mt. Everest of plays. What accounts for its unique prestige? How modern a play is <u>Hamlet</u>? What are the political issues raised by the play?

Video interview with:

Professor Mick Hattaway, University of Sheffield, author of a critical text on Shakespeare's <u>Hamlet</u>

III. VIDEOTAPE COMMENTARY

I suggest you read this section before you watch the videotape. You will find that it will help you organize your thoughts in a more useful way than if you just watch the tape "cold." When you have finished viewing the tape you may want to read this section again.

A.   *Initial class discussion*

I begin this section with a greeting from Stratford Upon Avon, Shakespeare's birthplace, followed by a short recapitulation of various kinds of approaches to heroism in Virgil and Dante. The battlefield for Dante is not outside but inside oneself. Moving from Dante to Shakespeare represents another great leap in time. Barbara M. compares Hamlet with Aeneas in his initial indecisiveness, but there is a difference between the two. Hamlet's indecisiveness is perhaps well advised, as he "finds his uncle in his father's favorite chair." I suggest that he is indecisive because he knows how difficult the problems are. Helen asks the important question why is Hamlet not the King. I respond by reinforcing the fact that Denmark had an elected not a hereditary monarchy, and the kingdom eventually goes to Fortinbras. The question throughout the play is whether Hamlet possesses the qualities needed to be the king.

B. Interview with Professor Mick Hattaway, Department of English, Sheffield University, England

I start with this theme: Does a good king have to be a good man? Can a bad man be a good king? Professor Hattaway says that Hamlet was described too much in terms of his personality, and not sufficiently in terms of the political context in which he lived. The council, after all, had decided that his uncle would be a better king than he would be, and this was a perfectly legitimate decision made by an electorate. Claudius, for his part, is a good peace maker. Hamlet, on the other hand, is obsessed with his private problems, and is able to act only compulsively. Claudius is apparently a more reasonable person, and as such more acceptable in the face of the political and military threat by Fortinbras.

Professor Hattaway then gives an intriguing account of a particular production of the play within the play, commonly called the mousetrap. In this production Claudius refused to admit his guilt. This is very different from most interpretations, when at the end of the mousetrap Claudius usually acknowledges his guilt, but as Professor Hattaway says, the text leaves the question open. All this reinforces the point I make earlier in the discussion that drama is the result of three things working together, the text, the actors, and the audience.

C. Final class discussion

I begin this segment by asking the question, "Why is Hamlet so famous?" Barbara M. observes that the pages are filled with universal wisdom, applicable to any time and place. This is certainly true, with Hamlet containing an incredible amount of quoted speeches and phrases. I lead the discussion toward the proposition that this is a play in which the difference between what is real and what seems to be real is the greatest challenge. The court scene with the king, the queen and the courtiers is what meets the eye, but there is murder, fratricide, incest, and duplicity of all sorts lurking just beneath the surface. I then ask if Hamlet appears as an adolescent in his behavior. Virginia agrees, saying that he constantly puts on facades for various people. He is not manipulative, but carefully plans to fulfill the burden put on him by his father's ghost. And what a mess, I observe, that he made of it! A lot of people die who do not deserve to die. He vacillates, and when he does make the decision he is rash. I ask if Hamlet has a tragic flaw, and if so, what is it? Charles suggests that it is introspection to the point of incapacitation. Agnes says that he was spoiled, that he was locked in an Oedipal struggle. He wanted his mother to be there for him.

The discussion then turned toward the language in Hamlet. People in the class found it rich, and that it worked best when they read it out loud. I agree, and point out that there are many puns in Hamlet, that he was a wonderful wordsmith. Language was in flux then, just as it is today. We often need a glossary to be given the true meaning of words which are archaic or obsolete. Mary says that he was an idealist, and that idealists can be very cruel, because they find something wrong with everybody because they fall short of what they ought to be. They have tunnel vision. I then ask if Hamlet undergoes any fundamental changes in the play, does he learn anything? For instance, his costume changes seem to have some significance. His dark ink-black clothes change to the regular clothes of a traveler. Early in the play he asks himself if he should live in the face of eternal disappointment, but in the gravediggers' scene he may have come to a different view.

The discussion then turns to who are the "actors" in the play. Certainly the women, Gertrude and Ophelia, are more acted upon than actors. The actors are the men. Hamlet's act is that he is acting. Fortinbras is important too. He is a man of action. Is the play endorsing leadership qualities? This leads to the question as to why Hamlet is given a soldier's burial. Why this seemingly undeserved reward? What is his war? The world in which Hamlet has to act is a fallen world. He must act in it, and what's more he must use the methods of that fallen world. He wants to act in an ideal world, which is an impossibility. The play suggests that the fight between good and evil is not a fair one. In the symbolic fight at the end of the play, the poisoned rapier is used by evil in the final scene, but it ultimately changes hands. Hamlet adopts the methods of the real world. Finally, we end the hour with the question, what has happened to Hamlet's perspective that allows him to duel with evil and to give his life for a cause? ♣

 *Now, please enjoy the videotape.*

IV. REVIEW QUESTIONS

1. Does Hamlet have a tragic flaw? If so, what is it?

2. Why does Hamlet delay so long in taking his revenge? Is this a weakness or a strength in Hamlet's character?

3. Trace a pattern of imagery in the play—disease, the garden, clothes, art or painting. How does this imagery advance the play's theme?

4. Who are the "actors" in the play?

5. Why does Hamlet receive a hero's burial? What about him is heroic?

V. FURTHER READING

NOTE: Because so much has been written about this play, it is difficult at best to list merely a few critical texts. For the beginning reader of Hamlet, I'd suggest these three collections of critical readings.

Hattaway, Michael. Hamlet: An Introduction to the Variety of Criticism. London: Macmillan, 1987.

Hoy, Cyrus. Hamlet (Norton Critical Edition). New York: W. W. Norton & Company, Inc., 1963.

Wofford, Susanne, L., ed. Hamlet (Case Studies in Contemporary Criticism). Boston: Bedford Books of St. Martin's Press, 1994.

NOTES

LESSON 13:   SHAKESPEARE, HAMLET, PART 2

 Before you read this chapter of the Study Guide

READ: Text: Maynard Mack, Ed., Norton Anthology of World
Masterpieces, vol. 1, pp. 2014-2110

I.   INTRODUCTION

You will see at the beginning of this lesson that I ask my students to be more "personal" in their responses to the play, i.e., not to respond to questions with received opinion—a pretty tough task when dealing with a play as well known as this one. In this lesson, we discuss several important themes: Hamlet's enigmatic character, his peculiar relationship with Gertrude, the play's modernity, and a feminist reading of the character and actions of Ophelia.

II.   VIDEOTAPE SYNOPSIS

This is a continuation of our discussion of the previous hour. In this hour we look at the political issues raised by the play. Later, a feminist and an existential reading of the play is offered for consideration by the class, i.e., the play evokes fears and disgust for the sexualized maternal body; and the play poses the question of how to act in the world when one cannot know anything with certainty.

Video interview with:

Professor Mick Hattaway, University of Sheffield, author of a critical text on Shakespeare's <u>Hamlet</u>

III.   VIDEOTAPE COMMENTARY

I suggest you read this section before you watch the videotape. You will find that it will help you organize your thoughts in a more useful way than if you just watch the tape "cold." When you have finished viewing the tape you may want to read this section again.

A.   *Initial class discussion*

I begin by reminding the class that they shouldn't approach Hamlet with kid gloves, that they shouldn't be afraid of it, in spite of its having acquired the kind of awesome respect that it wields as the best known play in English. Interpretation, after all, especially the interpretation of great works of art, is an on-going process which is to a large degree subjective.

We then move into a discussion of Hamlet's character, how he is plagued by his indecisiveness. Over and over in the play he upbraids himself for not acting. He wishes he were more like Laertes and Fortinbras. I suggest that part of Hamlet's problems is that he is still an adolescent, with a stark sense of right and wrong. It's hard to know what is from what seems. His procrastination stems from his desire to know the facts before he acts.

Chad suggests that he had a need to cling to his sense of duty. His father's ghost charges him to avenge him. Throughout the play Hamlet is struggling with his sense of duty as he had several opportunities to kill his uncle and yet he doesn't. Barbara M. asks the intriguing question as to whether Hamlet would have acted this way if there weren't a ghost, because when he came back he was not suspecting murder at the time, implying that if it weren't for the ghost, he would not have been bent on revenge.

Running with this, I ask the class, if you separate out the revenge factor, what is it that's bothering him? That his mother married his uncle? Susan suggests that her offense is that she has married so soon, a couple of months after his father's death. He calls it the incestuous relationship. This leads us into a lively discussion about how sons and daughters view their mothers, and how Gertrude was a lusty, physical woman.

We then move into a short technical interlude, prompted by Charles' asking what T. S. Eliot had meant when he called Hamlet the "Mona Lisa of literature." Eliot felt that we could not understand Gertrude because there was nothing in the play that helped us. He said this because Hamlet didn't have the objective correlative.

(I promised in the tape to explain in the Study Guide what an objective correlative is, so if you're interested, here it is!

"Objective Correlative" is a term first used by T.S. Eliot in his essay, "Hamlet and His Problems." Eliot writes that "the only way of expressing emotion in the form of art is by finding an 'objective correlative;' in other words, a set of objects, a situation, a chain of events which shall be the formula of that *particular* emotion; such that when the external facts, which must terminate in sensory experience, are given, the emotion is immediately invoked."

Eliot finds the objective correlative in what he calls "Shakespeare's more successful tragedies," but faults Hamlet for lacking it. He argues that "Hamlet (the man) is dominated by an emotion which is inexpressible, because it is in excess of the facts as they appear... Hamlet is up against the difficulty that his disgust is occasioned by his mother, but that his mother is not an adequate equivalent for it; his disgust envelops and exceeds her. It is thus a feeling which he cannot understand; he cannot objectify it, and it therefore remains to poison life and obstruct action." You should know that a veritable sea of ink has been published in the last sixty years or so disputing or developing Eliot's criticism of the play on this principle. What do you think?)

We then move to the actions of Gertrude and Claudius. I observe in their defense that Gertrude and Claudius must consolidate power, they are not just free beings, they represent the body politic. The body politic needs a head, and Claudius is the head. Eric suggests that although we understand that Claudius was chosen through a constitutional process, the popular sympathy was with Hamlet. I agree with him, but alert him to how Shakespeare treats the rabble in this play. There is this distrust of the rabble that is written into our culture. They can be swayed easily by demagogues. I bring back a point from the previous lesson, that popular or not, there are things about Hamlet's personality that would have made him probably unfit to be king. This is what Professor Hattaway asserted in the previous lesson, holding that Claudius was a good king, in spite of being a bad man. Which brings us back to the consideration of whether a good man by definition must make a good king. These issues are very modern.

We then explore the question of what is modern about this play. Virginia suggests that it's the background diplomacy, - "we only want to go through with our army because we are really attacking Poland." I agree that the power politics embedded in the play is one of the main modern themes. During this and subsequent discussions, I make reference to "Rosty," or Dan Rostenkowski. At the time of the discussion, he was Chairman of the House Ways and Means Committee, and a long-time Democratic representative from Chicago. At that particular time he was under fire for some postal irregularities, but the sense of the class was that he would ride out the storm. In the subsequent election, however, Rostenkowski was defeated by a virtually unknown Republican opponent. Barbara M. ends this discussion by observing that Hamlet would have made a terrible king, because he was ruled by passion and the impulse for revenge.

I pick up on the theme of what is modern about the play in the next episode.

B. Interview with Professor Mick Hattaway, Department of English, University of Sheffield, England

Professor Hattaway suggests that Hamlet is modern in all kinds of ways. Much of the play turns around the court which during Shakespeare's time was very important, in that the state is becoming more centralized. The play is thus modern in the sense that we are similarly obsessed with the growth of the state in our century. Another modern aspect is the fact that although Hamlet is about the ability to perceive the way that the world is moving, it equally leaves us with the feeling that it is very difficult to do anything about it.

I then ask is that what Hamlet wins to in the end, a better understanding of how the world actually works? Professor Hattaway thinks he does, but it's a very salutary lesson that he learns. He ends the interview by speculating on why in most productions Hamlet dies laughing.

C. Final class discussion

Barbara M. begins the discussion by observing that the play reinforces the feeling that there are forces at work in the world that are so hard to understand and how hard it is to control what you don't understand. I agree, and suggest that it takes a certain courage to act when you can't foresee the consequences, just as Aeneas had to. And for Hamlet, how hard it was to act in a world of seeming, to act in a world of actors, to play within a play. I then speculate on whether his acting, although it ends up in the death of so many people, is not perhaps why Hamlet gets the burial he gets at the end of the play. Maybe Hamlet really is heroic, maybe more so than his father. Perhaps the new battlefield is not that of Fortinbras but is the battlefield inside us.

Finally we turn to Ophelia, who is the other person who comes out of this play as famous as Hamlet. I observe that feminist critics have said that Ophelia's madness is a perfectly appropriate response to a world where she was constantly being used by men as a bargaining chip, where her fate is not in her hands but in those of the males around her. Valeria remarks how she found an ally in Gertrude who had hoped she would bear an heir for her. I agree and add that Ophelia did nothing to cause her downfall, that she did not act but was acted upon. There is one act she does take, however, the one act that is so defining, so existential—her act of suicide. Eric, however, puts a nice twist on this by observing that he got the feeling that she just falls into the stream. She didn't even act to save herself. Even her suicide is passive. Or ambiguous, I add.

Barbara M. steers the final discussion to what she observes as Hamlet's lack of emotion. Compared to Aeneas who expressed regret, Hamlet commits murder but doesn't have any feelings for it. Susan observes in Hamlet's defense, that Aeneas was a much older, more mature person. She also says that she has a problem with blaming Hamlet for Ophelia's death, because he didn't know about it until he came back from England, and was devastated by it. The class ends with some back and forth as to whether Hamlet showed enough grief for Ophelia's loss, and as I observe, we're left fittingly for a play where illusion and substance coexist side by side with "all these incoherent expressions of emotion." ♣

 *Now, please enjoy the videotape.*

IV. REVIEW QUESTIONS

1. How modern a play is <u>Hamlet</u>?

2. Why does Hamlet delay?

3. Is Hamlet's apparent madness real or feigned?

4. Consider the theme of the "sexualized maternal body" in <u>Hamlet.</u>

5. Is it necessary that the good political leader also be a good person? Why? Is Claudius a "good" king?

6. How do you view the ending of the play? Do you have a sense that all has been made well at the end of the play?

V. FURTHER READING

Please refer to the readings in Lesson 12.

LESSON 14:   MOLIERE, TARTUFFE

 Before you read this chapter of the Study Guide

READ: Text: Maynard Mack, Ed., Norton Anthology of World
Masterpieces, vol. 2, pp. 10-67

I.   INTRODUCTION

If ever a play demanded to be read aloud to hear the subtle rhythms and emphases of dialogue and speech, it is Tartuffe. Note the speed with which the lines of the play establish both character and action. As you read the play, try to imagine how the characters are grouped on the stage and how Moliere masterfully uses props and body language to comic effect—the "dance" of the two lovers whose pride almost causes their separation, Tartuffe admiring Elmire's bosom, Orgon hiding under the table. Don't lose sight of the fact that, as Professor David Raybin says on the videotape, despite being a classic this is a very funny play.

But its comedy is dark. Remember that while Tartuffe seems funny—even preposterous—to you as reader, to the people in the play he is a very real threat. He is the sinister outsider, without social context and without family or friends, who threatens to destroy the family. Orgon, a prisoner of his own ego needs, is all too willing to give Tartuffe what he wants: power and the necessary authority to execute it. Seen from this point of view, the "deus ex machina" ending may be more than an awkward way out of a plot difficulty or a piece of fulsome flattery of the King. Just as it looks as if the forces of evil will triumph at the end, chance steps in to save Orgon from himself. Even though he has seen Tartuffe for what he is, Orgon is powerless himself to rectify his past mistakes.

II.   VIDEOTAPE SYNOPSIS

The discussion centers on Tartuffe as a representative play of the French neo-classical period—especially its plot, language, characterization and theme. The key questions that we discuss are: what is the play about? Why is Orgon so blind to Tartuffe's true nature? Is the character of Tartuffe comic or macabre? Is Orgon "mad," as Dorine calls him? What does "madness" mean in the context of this play? What is the meaning of the "deus ex machina" ending of the play?

Video interview with:

Dr. David Raybin, Department of English, Eastern Illinois University

III.   VIDEOTAPE COMMENTARY

I suggest you read this section before you watch the videotape. You will find that it will help you organize your thoughts in a more useful way than if you just watch the tape "cold." When you have finished viewing the tape you may want to read this section again.

A.   Initial class discussion

I begin by remarking that it is quite a large leap, not so much in time, but in style of production when we move from Shakespeare's Hamlet with all of its psychological complexities, its depth of character, and its ambiguous world to the bright lights of neoclassic comedy in Moliere's <u>Tartuffe</u>. Neo-classic style is a tough form: students tend not to like it because it's artificial. As with classical drama, there is a unity of time, place and action. Rosemary likens it to one of Noel Coward's plays, which is a good analogy, as it is a comedy of manners, but a dark comedy. Virginia remarks that she finds it musical, which is an excellent point. I urge you to read this play aloud. The music of the language is obviously quite rhythmic. There is great repetition. The most obvious is Orgon coming home and being told that his wife's been sick in bed with a headache, and all he can say is, "And Tartuffe...? and Tartuffe....? and Tartuffe ....?"

Moliere's sense of the theater is perfect. In performance, <u>Tartuffe</u> is just amazingly funny stuff in spite of its heroic couplets. Barbara C. comments on the more serious aspects of the play, such as the negative criticisms of religion and the church. I agree that this was certainly a major criticism of the play. I then ask the class whether criticism of the church is what this play is about. Ada says that she wasn't offended about the reference to the church at all. She saw it as poking fun at hypocrisy, which is disdained in all circles of life. I agree that we do take a certain delight when religious hypocrites are exposed, giving the example of the famous television evangelist, Jimmy Swaggart. I then remark that the religious act is meaningless without knowing intention. This will be a central theme of this discussion. Moliere also took on the nobility, not just the clergy.

At this point I ask the key question: What does Orgon get from Tartuffe? Virginia says that because everyone around him is young, and he married a younger woman, he feels that he must fight to remain the head. Barbara M. suggests that if this were Shakespeare, the lovers would have been torn apart and the wife would have had the affair with Tartuffe, and she makes a good point. The play is about the uncovering of a sham. We laugh at Tartuffe, but his is a very dark character. He comes into the play without any human connection, except for his man servant, Laurent. In a daring piece of dramaturgy Moliere holds back Tartuffe's entrance until the middle of the play. I expect you noticed that. And then in a moment of brilliance, in comes Tartuffe yelling at the man servant, "Hang up my hair shirt!"

Chad then asks the question which is on the minds of a number of students as to what exactly was the relationship between Orgon and Tartuffe. He quotes two lines from Act 1, Scene 2, where Dorine says, "He calls him brother and loves him as his life,/preferring him to mother, child or wife./ He pets and pampers him with love more tender,/ than any petty mistress could engender." He suggests that Orgon may have a bit more for Tartuffe than religious admiration, that he may have a quasi-homosexual crush on him. Virginia agrees that he does have a crush on him but it is more like a crush a teenager might have than something sexual. At this point, I suggest that what Orgon is really about is his power in the family unit.

I then ask the "simple" question again: "What's this play about?" Agnes suggests that it's about family, power, and exposing the corruption of the nobility and clergy. I argue caution here, asking whether Tartuffe really represents the clergy.

I remind the class that the play is very clear, that one must not mistake act for meaning. You've got to know intention. If you remember, we talked about this with Oedipus. If you judge Oedipus' acts independent of motivation, then you say he's guilty of patricide and incest. But as soon as you look at motivation and intention, it's quite clear that he is guilty of neither. This play was written when the Age of Reason was coming into being, the age of Francis Bacon, the age of inductive reasoning, and people are starting to view the world differently from the old days when people went on processions and pilgrimages and performed symbolic acts.

B. *Video interview with Dr. David Raybin, Eastern Illinois University.*
I first asked him how the play was received in its time. Dr. Raybin said that initially it was banned

from public performance. Some people in the church complained that "Tartuffe" was an attack on the church. Moliere wrote a strong preface to the play, in which he argued against the complaint. He argued that it was so blatant about Tartuffe's hypocrisy, that we were prepared for it for two acts, that no one could imagine that this was an ordinary church figure, that he was a hypocrite, an evil man, and every audience would know this.

Dr. Raybin is a medievalist, a Chaucerian scholar. I then asked him as a medievalist to comment on the difference between intention and act. Dr. Raybin replied that Chaucer had a similar concern about intention and act. He gives the example of Madame Pernelle, Orgon's mother, who comes on stage chastising the family, the serving maid, everyone. She's worried about their behavior. If their behavior had been improper, this would have been reasonable. But since they have been behaving well, they haven't had bad intentions, there is nothing in their actions that ought to be condemned. At first we ourselves wonder who is wrong here, but Moliere makes it clear because he makes her so ludicrous.

We then turn to the contemporary applications of the play. Dr. Raybin suggests that the play is about authority, about growing older and what happens to us as we grow older. It's about what we do at moments when we are not sure of ourselves. In contemporary America a large number of people turn to people with deep charisma and deep power whom others would see as charlatans. What is contemporary about this play is that it examines why people allow themselves to be duped by others.

I then ask him what is the sting in this play. Dr. Raybin stresses that Orgon is a good man. He decided to help a friend in trouble, despite the fact that his friend had done disloyal acts. He refers to the poet, W. H. Auden, who says that if he had to choose between his friend and his country, he hoped he'd choose his friend, although he wasn't sure. He contrasts this with Creon in <u>Antigone</u> who says that he hoped he would never abandon his country for a friend. It is Orgon's very goodness that has put him in danger.

Finally, I ask him what is classic about <u>Tartuffe</u>. And Dr. Raybin makes the humorous reply that Moliere's plays are so good, that in spite of being called classics, we can still enjoy them.

C. *Final class discussion*

Barbara M. begins the discussion by commenting on Dr. Raybin's comparison of <u>Tartuffe</u> with <u>Antigone</u>. But here the king, unlike Creon, is wise enough and mature enough to realize that what is right has to be done sometimes. He's big enough of a royal to realize that his power is not being endangered. I remark that this "deus ex machina," (God out of the machine) ending is in obvious praise of Louis and his acumen, and his ability to see the right act even if it might not be the legal act.

Rosemary brings the discussion back to Orgon's "goodness." She thought of him as a good man and felt that he envied Tartuffe's seeming virtue and wanted to instill it in his own life. I agree that from the very first act it was established that Orgon is a good man, but as in more enduring pieces of literature, that goodness is complex. Unlike the world of melodrama, where the good is all good and the bad is all bad, I think that most of us are good people but we do fall trap to certain excesses.

Chad then brings up the character of Dorine, and how she tells Marianne to defy her father and not agree to marry Tartuffe against her wishes just to please her father. I see the Dorine character as being really fun, a character straight from our situation comedies. All around are pretentious, goofy, upper class people who need the commonsense and wit of this lower class person to bring them back to center. Valeria points out, however, that men still define women's roles. I agree, and suggest that the "pater familias" idea is almost abused to the point of tragedy. Orgon if left unchecked would have tyrannized that family.

We then get back to the central question as to why was Orgon so taken in? How can such a good, intelligent man get fooled so badly? And what is Orgon getting from Tartuffe? Susan suggests that it is reassurance, affirmation of his efforts to control his family. He is buying Tartuffe, and in so doing, he is buying power and control. He's aligning himself with Tartuffe's supposed spirituality, and lofty goals.

Finally I bring up the point that Dorine refers to Orgon as "mad" in the play. What is Orgon's madness? Barbara M. suggests that he has lost his reason and his heart too, in a way. I agree. Orgon has been tutored by Tartuffe to say that his wife, son, and daughter could die and he wouldn't feel a thing. The divine love that is supposed to motivate has been replaced by self-love. The play suggests just how destructive to the group that kind of self-love can be. It threatens to destroy the entire family. Ada quotes us a saying that fits in nicely in this context, that "you are becoming so heavenly minded, that you are of no earthly good." This is indeed the madness. So the play suggests sane moderation is healthy. Monomania can take many forms, in the 20th century it can be political, religious, ideological, economic. As we said at the beginning, this is a comedy, but a dark comedy. It leaves us with the final question, how do innocents keep going when that innocence is crushed by hypocrisy, how do we live a sane healthy life without cynicism? ♣

 *Now, please enjoy the videotape.*

IV. REVIEW QUESTIONS

1. Dorine calls Orgon "mad." Is he mad? What does madness mean in the context of the play?

2. Is Tartuffe a comic character? Is he comic in the same way Orgon is comic?

3. Why is Orgon so blind to Tartuffe's real nature?

4. Consider the role of power in this play. Who has it? Who hasn't? How should power best be exercised?

5. Comment on the "deus ex machina" ending. Does this ending have any thematic significance?

V. FURTHER READING

Gossman, L. Man and Masks. Baltimore, MD: Johns Hopkins Press, 1963.

Guicharnaud, J. ed. Moliere: A Collection of Critical Essays. Englewood Cliffs, NJ: Prentice-Hall, 1964.

Jagendorf, Zvi. The Happy End of Comedy. Newark, NJ: University of Deleware Press, 1984.

LESSON 15:   MILTON, PARADISE LOST, PART 1

 Before you read this chapter of the Study Guide

READ: Text: Maynard Mack, Ed., Norton Anthology of World
Masterpieces, vol. 1, pp. 2179-2208

I.   INTRODUCTION

If you are like most of the students in the teleclass, you will be coming to Milton for the first time. Again, like them, your initial impressions might have been that Paradise Lost is extraordinarily difficult to read and indeed alien to our world and times. I for my part can remember finding Milton boring, irrelevant, and almost unreadable when I read him for the first time in my sophomore survey course as an undergraduate. It was only after I had read him extensively that I could respond to the poetry of Milton - the sound, the rhythm, the extraordinary tonal effects, the striking juxtapositions of diction - for example, Satan standing "stupidly good." (I urge you to read Milton out loud to help you fully appreciate these cadences.) I have taught Milton courses for many years now, and it has been most encouraging over the years to see my students change from initial rejection to appreciation of what Milton has to say to us in our own journeys of self-exploration.

You will find, I'm sure, that coming to Milton after having read the Old Testament, Homer, Virgil and Dante will make Paradise Lost more accessible to you than it is for students who do not have that frame of reference. Indeed, you will notice this as the first classroom observation in this lesson. Milton quite consciously invites comparisons between his poem and these other texts. A useful exercise for you will be to stay alert to how Milton uses the so-called "great tradition" to his own ends.

Many of Milton's ideas are strikingly modern, especially his views on censorship, divorce, and education. But many are not. There is little doubt in the poem, for example, about the role of gender in fixing one's place in the scheme of things. Adam and Eve are not equals from this point of view. Yet, it is Eve who proves to be the hero of the poem. Similarly, Milton's views on freedom, the limits of knowledge, and the impossibility of separating spiritual values from natural values, to name but a few, strike the modern reader as old-fashioned.

But don't be too quick to dismiss him as antique. His insistence throughout the poem on the necessity of "decentralizing" the ego as the proper path toward a "Paradise within thee happier far" than the earthly paradise is well worth your serious consideration, as are the prescriptions given Adam by both Raphael and Michael. Ultimately, this is a poem about nothing less than the "best" way to live one's life. It is not so much motivated by the need for self-expression (as so much modern poetry is) as it is designed to engage the audience in a deep and meaningful examination of both the inner- and outer-directed life.

One final note. Try to read the whole poem. Doing so will certainly make my comments in class more meaningful, just as it will make my video-guest, Dr. Falconer's, insights more telling.

II.   VIDEOTAPE SYNOPSIS

What is Milton's purpose in singling out the myth of Adam and Eve for such extended attention? What is heroism and who is heroic by Milton's standards? What is "innocence" according to

Milton? Is it a desirable trait? What is the role of knowledge in the epic? What does it mean to "be lowly wise?" Of particular attention is the question of Eve as champion of <u>Paradise Lost.</u>

Video interview with:

Dr. Rachel Falconer, University of Sheffield, Sheffield, England

III. VIDEOTAPE COMMENTARY

I suggest you read this section before you watch the videotape. You will find that it will help you organize your thoughts in a more useful way than if you just watch the tape "cold." When you have finished viewing the tape you may want to read this section again.

A. *On location introduction*

I begin the class with a brief introduction from the garden of Milton's cottage at 21 Deans Way, Chalfont St. Giles, in Buckinghamshire, about 35 miles north-west of London. This was the house which Milton retreated to in 1665 to escape the great plague, and it now houses a Milton museum. I strongly recommend a visit to this museum, although be sure not to go in the dead of winter as we were forced to do, when the museum was unfortunately inaccessible to visitors.

B. *Opening class discussion*

As usual, I look to the class participants to set the pattern for the opening discussion. Virginia begins by saying how useful it was to come to Milton after reading the other classics, especially the <u>Aeneid</u> and Dante, because without that background Milton would have been even harder to read. I agree with her that Milton is indeed difficult to read, as I'm sure you will have discovered for yourself by now. Milton did not write for everybody: he sought a "fit audience though few." However, the more learning you bring to the poem, the more the poem gives you back.

Barbara C. now turns the topic towards the character of God, whom she finds disturbingly inconsistent. As she observes, He forgives the angels when they let the serpent sneak in, but He throws Adam and Eve out. He has the ability to see the future and yet He never tries to change it. I refer her to Book III, where Milton introduces God as a character, which is one of the most controversial inventions of Milton. Indeed some would argue that Milton made a big mistake in doing this, because it is very difficult, if not impossible, to present God as a character without having that character not appear in some way self-limiting, or foolish, or offensive. Milton's God is a very legalistic deity, He's a very harsh deity, and a frighteningly egotistical deity.

Some of the class have trouble with the discrepancies between the characters in the Book of Genesis, especially God and Satan, and the characters that Milton has turned them into. I remind the class that Milton has taken the story contained in one fairly small chapter, Genesis III, and has from this invented a twelve-book epic, and thus he has taken considerable liberties in fleshing out the main characters. Which brings up the interesting question for us as to why someone would take Genesis 3 and make a heroic poem out of it?

We then follow with some discussion about the nature of an epic, and we revisit the theme as to why Milton insisted on making his epic so difficult to read. When it first came out, people objected to it on any number of levels, not the least of which was the fact that it didn't rhyme. He appended to the title page of the second edition a rather large poem by Andrew Marvell, where Marvell defends the fact that it is not rhyming. Milton adds a note to the reader, beginning "The measure is English heroic verse without rhyme." He's a very confrontational, argumentative man.

In answer to Barbara M.'s question about how people responded to the book since unlike Dante who had selective targets, Milton seemed to be tilting at the whole world, I give a fairly lengthy summary of his personal development from child to man and the political background in which Milton was writing. Besides being a poet, Milton was very active in the world of politics, and held a high position under Oliver Cromwell, the person who overthrew the Royalists in the Civil War and had King Charles I executed in 1649. In fact, Milton became the spokesman for the revolution, writing among other things a defense for the execution of the King, at a time when regicide (the killing of a king) in the Renaissance was tantamount to killing God's representative, as Kings were held to rule by Divine Right. It was a very dangerous thing to do, and when the Restoration of the monarchy came in 1660 with the accession to the throne of King Charles II, son of King Charles I, some old debts were settled - Cromwell's body, for instance, was exhumed and publicly hanged - and Milton was lucky to escape execution himself.

This seething political period surfaces in many ways in <u>Paradise Lost</u> where you will see all sorts of slams against the monarchy and tyranny, against people in positions of power, people who abuse that power, the corrupted clergy. He was also very disrespectful towards women which leads me to ask the question as to why we are enjoying a renaissance of interest in Milton, why do we read this incredibly difficult poem that puts women down at almost every turn? We will get more insight on this question in the video-interview later on in the lesson.

We then turn to the matter of Milton's inspiration. He knew from quite early on that he had been called to write an epic. His nephew, Edward Phillips, in his biography talks about how Milton as soon as he woke up composed whole chunks of verse. Milton believed it was God speaking through him. He believed in that old classical tradition of the poet as "vates" or prophet.

Rosemary turns the discussion back to the character of Satan, which she finds immensely disturbing, as he is so unlike the "real" Satan from the Bible. Again, as when we were reading the book of Genesis, I ask you to try not to let your own belief system prevent you from taking seriously the story of Adam and Eve, as Milton has told it. Milton's Satan is really fantastic, and not at all melo-dramatic. He is one of the most complex characters you will ever meet. He is pathetic in many situations, and he is an admirable character in many ways. He is very much a heroic character. He is not a cardboard Satan. He feels compassion for his fellows, - and it's not a sham compassion, as Rosemary suggests, but a real compassion. He does feel for his fellows. He feels responsible for their situation, and he feels the guilt for that quite enormously. Milton makes him a complex charac-ter, otherwise there is no conflict, otherwise it is a melodrama and not an epic. You are supposed to feel sympathy for Satan. At this point Chad remarks how surprised he was to find himself having sympathy for the devil!

Virginia reads a passage early in Book I

> So stretcht out huge in length the Arch-fiend lay
> Chain'd on the burning Lake, nor ever thence
> Had ris'n or heav'd his head, but that the will
> And high permission of all-ruling Heaven
> Left him at large to his own dark designs,
> That with reiterated crimes he might
> Heap on himself damnation, while he sought
> Evil to others, and enrag'd might see
> How all his malice serv'd but to bring forth
> Infinite goodness, grace and mercy shewn
> On Man by him seduc't"

As Virginia observes, the justification was in the beginning: you saw Satan in his torment knowing that what was going to happen would be good in spite of himself. I respond by saying that that's how Milton creates the dramatic irony in the poem. I refer to the concept of the "felix culpa," the fortunate fall. From this fall will come the Christ figure. The interesting question in the epic is what's going to happen to Adam and Eve. In terms of the epic, the Christ figure is possible only if Adam and Eve reconcile. There will be no future for human kind, if Adam and Eve don't establish some kind of creative future for themselves. We will take up this issue in the video-interview in the next section.

C. Interview with Dr. Rachel Falconer, Department of English, University of Sheffield

I begin rather aggressively by observing that Paradise Lost has been dismissed by many people as a monument to dead ideas. This naturally draws a spirited response, in which Dr. Falconer states that Milton has written his poem in terms that we have the potential to fall or the potential to recover, that it speaks to all of us now, and is not merely a Biblical, crusty old poem.

We then turn to the subject of Eve, who is a controversial figure for modern students, especially when she is associated with such phrases as "he for God and she for God in him," which causes a groan from most contemporary student audiences. Dr. Falconer replies that Milton changed the story he inherited from Genesis by making Eve the central character of the poem. In effect he has rewritten the idea of epic by putting a woman in the center of action. "Maybe it's my prejudice, but I tend to see the fall of Eve as the central moment, and the recovery mediated through Eve, rather than through Adam, as the other central moment in the poem. So he has gone to extraordinary lengths to give her a central place, but I'm not sure it's from feminist instincts. I think that he has to create a new Eve, one who is worthy not to fall in order to justify God. Because, if he does create an Eve who is going to fall anyway, then in a way you can blame God for making her like that."

Finally, we talk about the nature of epics and how epics are generally built on a central heroic action. However, it is not clear what that might be in Paradise Lost. Dr. Falconer agrees that it is very difficult to locate the central event. If indeed it is the fall, the problem becomes that of where is the fall? "Is it Adam's fall because he is the head of the human race? Or is it Eve's fall, which is really the fall of man, because afterwards it seems more inevitable that both will fall? Or is it before that when she is tempted by Satan? Or is it before that when Satan is thrown out of heaven? And if the fall is that, then how do you explain that first fall, how is sin even conceived of?" However, she goes on to state that the very lack of center becomes very important in reading the poem, in fact it makes it a part of our own lives because the fall can happen to us anytime. It's happening to us as we read the poem and we're also looking for ways of recovering from it.

D. Final class discussion

The discussion focuses on free will. I give the class the caveat that they should not confuse fore-knowledge with predestination. This is a big distinction. Simply because God knew it was going to happen, doesn't mean God made it happen. Milton is very careful in Book III to make God distance himself from this type of inevitability. If Adam, Eve and Satan are puppets with God pulling the strings, then obviously this becomes a completely different epic. For reason to be meaningful in any way, it must be freely expressed. God himself says, if they're forced to obey, what kind of obedience is that? In order for it to be obedience, it must be chosen.

We then turn to another important idea of Milton, the concept of temptation. He writes in Areopagitica the most famous defense of freedom of the press and publication in Western culture, arguing that even bad books or seditious books should be published. "Let them grapple in the marketplace of ideas." He uses a wrestling metaphor, and good ideas will always win out over bad ones. He says, "I cannot praise a fugitive and cloistered virtue which dares not sally forth to meet its adversary." It's the notion that temptation is utterly important to leading a moral life, you do not withdraw from the world, you go out into the world. The central idea in Book III is the exercise of reason in the face of temptation that will bring you to reward.

We end the discussion by considering Adam's relationship with Eve. After the fall Adam is just vicious in his rebuking of Eve in Book X and he is willing to turn his back on her. However, Milton really does reinvent her, because she is the one who is most Christ-like after the fall. At the moment of Adam's rejection when he is filled with anger and hate, she does not answer anger with anger, she says "Forsake me not thus, Adam." She answers the vitriol with love. And it is that love that allows them to create a future and allows them to become aware that they have nobody else to blame but themselves. Peter asks the intriguing question as to what Milton would have had Adam do, if he weren't locked in to the story line. Would he have had him, like Aeneas, turn his back on his love? I reply by saying that the contrary might be the case, that the English essayist, C. S. Lewis, said that Adam was guilty of uxoriousness, that is, excessive love of one's spouse. In the middle books Adam complains about how lonely he is. Lewis wants to blame Adam for choosing Eve over following God's injunction. Adam knew what he was doing, he knew the consequences.

I end by saying that what gives me difficulty is this metaphor of a fall. I actually see it as a rise into a new kind of awareness, a new kind of adulthood, a new kind of humanity. To paraphrase the last line of the epic "with wandering steps and slow we make our solitary way." ♣

 ***Now, please enjoy the videotape.***

IV. REVIEW QUESTIONS

1. Describe in detail the characteristics of Milton's style in Paradise Lost. Give examples to illustrate.

2. What is "innocence?" Is it a desirable trait? How powerful is innocence against evil?

3. In Book I, lines 254-55, Satan asserts "The mind is its own place, and in itself/ Can make a Heaven of Hell, a Hell of Heaven." Does your reading of Paradise Lost support this assertion?

4. Epics are centered upon a hero performing a heroic action. What is the heroism and who is the hero of Paradise Lost?

5. What is the dramatic and thematic significance of Adam and Eve's reconciliation in Book X?

V. FURTHER READING

Barker, Arthur E., ed. <u>Milton: Modern Essays in Criticism</u>. New York: Oxford University Press, 1965

Demaray, John G. <u>Milton's Theatrical Epic: The Invention and Design of Paradise Lost</u>. Cambridge, Mass: Harvard University Press, 1980

Elledge, Scott., ed. <u>Paradise Lost</u>. New York: W.W. Norton and Co., 1975

Fish, Stanley E. <u>Surprised by Sin</u>. London: Macmillan Press, 1967

Wittreich, Joseph Anthony. <u>Feminist Milton</u>. Ithaca, NY: Cornell University Press, 1987

NOTES

LESSON 16: MILTON, PARADISE LOST, PART 2

☞ **Before you read this chapter of the Study Guide**

READ: Text: Maynard Mack, Ed., Norton Anthology of World
Masterpieces, vol. 1, pp. 2208-2221

I. INTRODUCTION

I again encourage you to read more of the epic than the scant selection in the Norton anthology. What do you make of the relation between the sexes in Paradise Lost? Is it realistic—even today? Do Adam and Eve's dialogues strike you as contemporary or hopelessly old-fashioned? When Eve rails against marriage as an institution—perhaps the first time this is done in Western literature—does she sound contemporary? Is her relationship with Adam based upon power before the Fall? What replaces "power" in the relationship after the fall? Would you want to live in Paradise?

II. VIDEOTAPE SYNOPSIS

Our discussion in Part II of Paradise Lost picks up on several threads from Part I—the character of Satan, Eve as hero, the "felix culpa" (or fortunate fall) and Milton's purpose in writing the epic.

Video interview with:

Dr. Rachel Falconer, Dept. of English, University of Sheffield, Sheffield, England

III. VIDEOTAPE COMMENTARY

I suggest you read this section before you watch the videotape. You will find that it will help you organize your thoughts in a more useful way than if you just watch the tape "cold." When you have finished viewing the tape you may want to read this section again.

A. Initial classroom discussion

I begin by reading out the opening to Paradise Lost. I then comment on the elaborate syntax of Milton's sentences. The first sentence is sixteen lines long, with the verb coming in line 6. The first lines state the theme of the poem. I refer to other epics which also name the theme in the opening - "Menis" in the Iliad - "wrath," the anger of Peleus' son; or Virgil's beginning in the Aeneid, "Arma virumque cano," I sing of arms and the man. Milton does the same thing here. "Of man's first disobedience....and the fruit of that forbidden tree." The fruit might be the consequence of that disobedience, the fruits of our labor.

The epic questions whether Adam and Eve are better in a moral sense after the fall than before. In Book XII Adam (after he's told of the "felix culpa" and of what the Christ figure represents) will wonder how to view his own disobedience. He's confused. He doesn't know whether to be happy or sad, and that's pretty much our condition as well. Traditionally we mourn the loss of Eden, but since the Renaissance we question whether it was the inevitable and good thing to do.

I then go on to discuss the seeking of knowledge, which caused the fall. It is quite clear that in the traditional scheme of things knowledge is a bad thing. Knowledge leads to suffering, we are better off in our innocence. The fall here is from innocence to experience. Adam and Eve don't gain abstract knowledge, they gain experiential knowledge. The movement this epic charts is the same that Genesis 3 charts: innocence to experience. Our condition is the condition of fallen Adam and Eve. Given that as our premise, how are we to live? Are we to long for a time of paradise, as a place, or are we to recreate paradise in our lives, and if so, how do we do it? That's what this epic is all about. One of the problematic things for a man as learned as Milton is the view of knowledge. Do we all know that knowledge is a dangerous thing? Michael says to Adam "Be lowly wise." In the middle books you see Adam speculating about the planets and astronomy. Raphael has to remind him that his realm of knowledge is on Earth and not up in the skies. Keep focused on how you live your life and don't spend time on idle speculation.

I then refer to Book 1 where the angels on the burning lake group themselves, there is one warrior group writing epic, singing of their battle in heaven. Another group are philosophers spending a lot of time in endless speculation, but their premise is flawed. The line I was searching for is:

> In discourse more sweet
> (For eloquence the soul, song charms the sense,)
> Others apart sat on a hill retired,
> In thoughts more elevate, and reasoned high
> Of providence, foreknowledge, will, and fate,
> Fixed fate, free will, foreknowledge absolute,
> And found no end, in wandering mazes lost.
> Of good and evil much they argued then,
> Of happiness and final misery,
> Passion and apathy, and glory and shame,
> Vain wisdom all, and false philosophy:

Science was just being born in this age and Milton is seeing a potential threat here. Susan comments that it was an exciting time for science then and it is now. But why is it that it is so hard to apply it for the betterment of humanity? I caution her on promoting just "useful" or potentially beneficial science, and remind her that we are cursed or blessed with an extraordinary imagination to ask those questions and we have to come up with answers to those questions. Rosemary then reminds us that the original sin was not so much seeking knowledge but disobedience, which prompts me to retort that one wonders what kind of a God it is who would create a garden and human beings with the nature they have, then create a situation in which they would behave in the way they did, and then punish them for it. This was Empson's point of view, that the real tyrant here is not Satan, but God who would do such a thing. (William Empson was an English Literature scholar of considerable reputation. Author of Seven Types of Ambiguity and other famous books, he was an outspoken critic of Milton's God and Christian theology in general. He was a counterbalancing force to C. S. Lewis' Christian apologetics.)

Barbara M. says that this is supported by Satan's argument to Eve, that if God is just, then nothing can happen to you. Barbara C. sees leaving paradise as a positive step in order to develop an inner paradise. I agree. Milton is suggesting what the church used to call heresy, which is that heaven and hell are not so much places, although they are useful for narrative, but they really are psychological states of mind. Satan says, "Wherever I go is hell, myself am hell." Because of this intellectual state, call it pride or egotism, whatever is motivating him, even in heaven it is a hell for him. "Better to rule in hell than serve in heaven," Satan says, a powerful line.

Please note in Book IX that Adam and Eve are always hand in hand. When they go their separate ways it is the first step towards their fall. Eve suggests that they divide their labors, a perfectly rational thing to do. (Valeria suggests that Eve felt too confined.) In Books XI and XII (not in the anthology), Adam and Eve are instructed by Michael in what virtues they need. There's a dual Trinity at work in the battlefield of Adam and Eve's heart and soul: the heavenly Trinity of God the Father, God the Son, and God the Holy Spirit. There's also an infernal Trinity: Satan, Sin and Death. Sin, who sprung whole from Satan's head, was his daughter. He then rapes his daughter, and Death is born. And who is going to make up the Trinity in Paradise, is it going to be Adam, Eve and Satan, or Adam, Eve and Christ? Adam and Eve must come together to make that third person of the Trinity possible. I can't stress this enough. If they do what Adam wants after the fall, then he makes Satan possible. But who is it that makes Christ and love and a future possible? It's Eve reaching out to Adam.

B. *Interview with Dr. Rachel Falconer, Department of English, University of Sheffield, Sheffield, England*

I remark that each of us could write our own experience with the fall, and ask her to talk to us about knowledge. Dr. Falconer responds that Satan uses this in the temptation scene - how can you possibly know what evil is and avoid it unless you know it? In terms of ourselves, as fallen readers, and in terms of Eve as someone who wants to seek out conflict, it's really a much more difficult point to challenge. In Areopagitica, Milton says it's the doom that we have fallen into since the fall to know our good by evil. Then he advises that we publish all kinds of books, so that we can explore all of the options before knowing what the truth is. And this is what Eve wants to do in Book IX. She's actually intrigued by Satan's ideas and dialogue, not by flattery.

I then suggest that we all experience being kicked out of the garden, that we often are led to think that life is meaningless, and ask how Paradise Lost speaks to this. Dr. Falconer responds that it corresponds very much to the low points in our own lives. The strength for Eve is the ability to look outwards when everything in your experience is looking inwards. Milton is extremely confrontational, he likes a good fight. He is extraordinarily open-minded, willing to hear other people's opinions. As an extension of that, the bitterness all gets directed outwards, which is healthier than letting it eat at you.

C. *Final class discussion*

Barbara M. wonders why Eve was not shown the vision of the future. She has demonstrated her independence and wisdom. Is she being punished? Or are they not giving her the mentality to cope with the vision that is shown to Adam? I reply that it was probably the latter; Michael's appeal is to Adam, the head of the family, not to Eve. Ada reminds us that Eve does come to know the future through dreams, so she's not left out entirely. I add that Milton admires Adam and Eve, because they are willing to go on, even after Adam has seen the grim vision of the future. The question is how to live in a fallen world? I direct the class's attention to the last lines of the poem. Eve says to Adam "Without thee here to stay is to go unwilling./ Thou to me art all things under heaven, all places thou." "Though all by me is lost (paradise)..by me the promised seed shall all restore." That word "seed" is repeatedly mentioned in Book XII, because that is her real blessing. The promise is on the creative future and Eve's role. "They hand in hand with wandering steps and slow,/ through Eden took their solitary way." It's a victory, not a moment of death. ♣

 *Now, please enjoy the videotape.*

IV. STUDY QUESTIONS

1. Characterize Milton's God. Is he an attractive character?

2. Who is the hero of <u>Paradise Lost</u>? Why?

3. Does Satan have a tragic flaw in the epic? Or is Satan pathetic rather than tragic? Explain.

4. Are the major issues of the epic resolved at the end?

V. FURTHER READING

I suggest you add these books to those listed in Class 15.

Hunter, G.K. <u>Paradise Lost</u>. London: G. Allen and Unwin, 1980.

McColley, Diane Kelsey. <u>Milton's Eve</u>. Urbana, IL: University of Illinois Press, 1983.

NOTES

LESSON 17:   VOLTAIRE, CANDIDE

    Before you read this chapter of the Study Guide

READ: Text: Maynard Mack, Ed., Norton Anthology of World
Masterpieces, vol. 2, pp. 336-402

I.   INTRODUCTION

You certainly don't need me to tell you that <u>Candide</u> is one of the funniest pieces of fiction you will ever read. The story's tone, improbable plot twists and turns, its unforgettable gallery of characters and settings all combine to make <u>Candide</u> one of the most famous works in western literature. Its satiric targets are so many and so seemingly contemporary—social injustice, religious oppression, legal corruption, court flattery, tyranny, snobbery, greed, and stupidity to name but a few—that it is as relevant to today's reader as it was in the 18th century.

But <u>Candide</u> is also very serious, perhaps among the most serious pieces of fiction ever written. Frederick the Great described it as "Job in modern dress." And, indeed, like the <u>Book of Job,</u> <u>Candide</u> clearly addresses the question of theodicy: why does evil exist in the universe? Why does the good man suffer? What is the relation of God to mankind? Does the cosmos run according to some rational scheme comprehensible to the human mind?

In its broadest sense, the subject of <u>Candide</u> is innocent man's experience of a mad and fallen world—his struggle to survive in that world, eventually to come to terms with it and to create his own existence within it. Like Adam and Eve before him, <u>Candide</u> is "kicked out" of an earthly paradise (a garden) and is forced to make the journey we all make from innocence to experience.

Finally, the lesson of <u>Candide</u> is worth your very serious consideration. There is no verbal, which is to say intellectual, solution to the problem of evil in the world or to the question of theodicy. Metaphysics is a delusion. Meaning is to be found only in socially productive work. We must cultivate our garden. And only we can do that.

A final personal note: I was fortunate enough to attend the 50 Year Commemoration Ceremonies of the Liberation of Auschwitz in 1995. It was a chilling and terrible experience to walk through Birkenau and Auschwitz in the dead of winter, to sense everywhere the fear and horror and degradation that were the normal lot of those condemned to die there. The one piece of literature that I most thought of during that week in Auschwitz was <u>Candide</u>. Is it any wonder?

II.   VIDEOTAPE SYNOPSIS

Is <u>Candide</u> "Job in modern dress," as Frederick the Great asserted? What is the theme of <u>Candide</u>? What is Voltaire's attitude toward metaphysical speculation? What is the role of work in <u>Candide</u>? Class focus is on the concept of the "garden" in the work, particularly the symbolic gardens, or ways of life, culminating in the three which rapidly succeed one another at the very end. The class is asked to consider <u>Candide</u> as a work following in the tradition of humankind's existential dilemma of finding meaning in a mad and evil world and creating meaningful existence within it.

Video interview with:
Professor Robert Morrissey, University of Chicago

III. VIDEOTAPE COMMENTARY

I suggest you read this section before you watch the videotape. You will find that it will help you organize your thoughts in a more useful way than if you just watch the tape "cold." When you have finished viewing the tape you may want to read this section again.

A. *Initial class discussion*

My first question was to ask how did Candide read? Chad said that he found it simple, easy to read and at first could not believe that it was a classic. I agree that it's quite a page turner at first. But usually by about the third chapter you have worked out the fact that there is an enormous gap between the form and the content. You're dealing with satire, an almost vicious kind of irony. Barbara 1. found it very concise and witty. Valeria remarked that you get the sense of the satire from Pangloss's name, "all is gloss." And Candide has such devotion to him no matter what happens. I agree that this is one of Candide's most attractive characteristics. Unlike Candide, when we get kicked out of the garden, we do not go through life expecting only good things to happen to us. The question is why does Candide go on? Virginia likens it to the quest for the Holy Grail. He must pursue it, when others would be content with what they have. I suggest that an ideal is driving him. He is reaching for something that is beyond his grasp, and that may be an important element in the story. I refer to the irony, which I hope you also noticed, of Candide's reunion with Cunegonde. She is not exactly what he left behind.

I then ask if people in the class see Eldorado as a positive ideal. Susan remarks that he leaves Eldorado, an earthly paradise, for her. Eldorado seems like a positive alternative to the kinds of brutality he talks about. Barbara M. suggests that he leaves Eldorado, just as Adam leaves Paradise, for his love. But Eldorado is more than a paradise. The people there think a little more and give thanks to God for what they have. Compared to the rest of the world, it certainly is a paradise. At this point I play the Devil's advocate and suggest that Eldorado, rather than being a paradise is actually hell. Eldorado is about the best description of hell that I have ever heard, where all our wants are satisfied, where we don't want for anything.

Helen remarked that the irony was really powerful. The philosophers could argue the grandeur of war, but on the other side, the spiritual values of war are wrong. And yet the king sang the "Te Deum" during the battle scene. It shows the hypocrisy of the church. Barbara M. asks why Voltaire doesn't say "Change the world, but accept what you can't change!"? Chad asks what it means when in Chapter 19 Martin, the philosopher, is first accused of being a Sochinian and then later a Manichean. I explain that these are known as two heresies in the church several hundred years before the writing of Candide. Voltaire was a very active man at court, and it's no surprise that, as did Dante, he would attack those who were against him. Peter says that he couldn't find anyone that Voltaire would respect. He was an iconoclast. It seems that he would criticize any mainstream class or idea.

I state that this is one of the criticisms of Candide. Voltaire has been accused of wretched pessimism, he is very ready to tear things down, but he has nothing to put up. So I ask whether the class can suggest any "positives" in this story? Barbara M. doesn't see it as negative. In the end he says "Cultivate your garden!" Again, playing the Devil's advocate, I suggest that this is self-indulgent, that it is no less than cowardice to make a conscious attempt to stay out of the marketplace of ideas.

B. *Interview with Professor Robert Morrissey, University of Chicago*

I ask him to put the work in context in Voltaire's life. Dr. Morrissey responds that it is a negative reflection of another work, published in 1747, Zadig, which has the same kind of epic journey. Zadig triumphs in the end due to friendship and love. However, in the ten years since Zadig, Voltaire was very active at court. When we come to Candide, Voltaire's private life is not going as well as he would have liked, and he's in disfavor with the court. Also in the interim there has been a massive earthquake in Lisbon. The dark side of the Enlightenment is beginning to surface now. Philosophers are beginning to question the early optimism that pervaded the Enlightenment. Rousseau has a whole series of questions that focus on the fundamental assumptions of the Enlightenment. I ask him if Candide, which Frederick the Great described as "Job in modern dress," is really about theodicy. Is that the central question of Candide? Professor Morrissey agreed that Candide questions the role of evil in the world. He's trying to come to some kind of answer as to what man can do in the world, what are the limits of our action and thought.

C. Final class discussion

I asked the class if they noticed how Dr. Morrissey set out the conflict between thought and deed. This will come up more and more, the need for action if we are going to make anything of life. Barbara M. interjected that cultivating your garden doesn't mean it has to be a plot of land. I agree that a garden is not a literal garden. It is any creative, productive work. I then go on to state that so many people thought theodicy was central to this work. The notion is that there is a good and just God, but there is a lot of evil in the world being visited indiscriminately on the good and bad. In the world of Candide there is the physical evil, the Lisbon earthquake or a storm at sea, something quite beyond any person's control. Then there is the social evil, which you see at every turn, such as syphilis. And then there is the personal evil of person against person. Evil is everywhere in this piece. We struggle to see the positive. Flaubert described this work as "a gnashing of teeth." Valeria observes that Candide was written at the beginning of the Enlightenment when man thought he could answer all questions in science. Voltaire was disillusioned that man couldn't answer all those questions.

Susan remarks that with Job, it was one man's personal struggle with things that kept happening. With Candide, it didn't seem to matter where he went or what he tried. He found evil everywhere he went, with the exception of Eldorado. I suggest that this is definitely what is known in literature as the "homo viator," man as wayfarer. It's the trip back that is especially interesting.

I then turn to the ending. I describe it as opening outwards when you compare the three gardens. There is Cacambo's garden, which is miserable, with no sense of purpose to the work at all. Then Candide visits the Old Turk's garden which gets a little larger. This time it's a family unit which is functioning quite well, although the Turk definitely turns his back on the world with philosophic disdain. The point is, does cultivating the garden do something positive for us, or does it merely serve to keep us from the negative? The Old Turk has a deistic view of the world. When asked whether he worries about the world, he says "Does the captain worry about the rats on the ship?" The notion of deism is that the world is created and God withdraws from it. The last garden is obviously more than a garden, because of the roles people are playing, with for instance Cunegonde becoming a pastry chef. But what happens when a little hierarchical ugliness raises its head? Valeria suggests that with that hierarchical arrangement you would want someone like Virgil at the head, and not Pangloss, someone who knows about the world and operates from reason, not just glossing over life. However, I counter that Pangloss is indeed not in charge. But Pangloss (the best of all possible worlds), Martin (the worst of all possible worlds), and Candide (the ameliorist in the middle), all have their place.

But what, I ask, is Candide doing in the garden? What is his job? You can tell me about all the others, but not those three I have just mentioned. This work seems to hold us in the 20th century because it seems to come so close to life as we know it. Ada contributes the adage that you should live each day as if it's your last and plan as if you would live forever. Valeria observes that before the Age of Enlightenment, theology was saying to man that God created an ordered universe. Now it's up to us with our free will to try to maintain an order on Earth.

I add that one of the things that keeps Candide going is hope and love. It is a terribly pessimistic work, but you do see a redemptive quality in hope and love. If we must cultivate our garden, why? In hope of what? What do we end up with? Happiness might be the Devil's invention. Reading this book makes you realize that life can make nonsense of your happiness at any moment. Is the happiness then in the pursuit rather than in the achieving?

We then discuss in more detail Eldorado. Virginia suggests that this wasn't happiness. They were complacent. This was a state of mind. I agree and add that they were afraid they would be like everyone else if they stayed there. They did not want to be like everyone else. Susan, however, disagrees. In her mind they weren't without intellect or in a state of ennui. She would have liked to know what else was going on in Eldorado. There were some wonderful things there - a lack of brutality and inhumanity to your fellows that was a stark contrast to what he encountered everywhere else. To her that's a desirable contrast. I suggest that the Eldorado dream was a motivator, but it is so unreal. Eric, however, doesn't see it as unreal. We could organize ourselves this way but we don't. The sense he has of Eldorado is the isolation from the world where his love is. If you are going to find Eldorado, you have to do it in a way that is connected with the world in a way that Eldorado is not.

I then ask again, what does it mean to cultivate our garden? Barbara M. thought that he's satirizing love because Candide goes through all these tribulations to find Cunegonde and when he gets her, he really doesn't want her. Voltaire is saying, "Be careful of what you love because you might get it!" Ada suggests that each man works out his own salvation and hopefully his God is strong enough and sufficient for the day.

I then ask if the work in our garden has to be practical, does it need to have a harvest? Susan wonders about this, citing Thomas Merton, the Trappist monk, who was a contemplative, but whose works have touched her. However, as I point out, his writing was his harvest, just as Voltaire's was. It's not enough to be contemplative. Chad remarks that they didn't emphasize what the garden produced, but rather their roles in it. I counter that when you see the succession of gardens, and you see the Old Turk's garden, you see that the product is important. He is taking his product and marketing it in the world. So don't focus in isolation on simply the last garden. If you work in a garden, it's got to issue in something, and what are you going to do with it? Chad agrees, but adds that as important as the product may be, it's also important to do the work in the garden. I translate this into meaning that instead of scientific speculation, Voltaire wants applied science.

Susan follows this up by saying that we need to keep in mind what our own products are. As a nation our main exports are arms. This is a good point, and I use it to emphasize that you very easily find modern applications for this work. What is poignant about it is what has happened to the quality of our work. In the last garden there is a much more intimate connection between one's labor and the product of one's labor. But for most of us who work in enormously complex systems, the work is alienating. In short, work is not an end in itself, but it becomes a means for producing capital. "The nature of work," as you will see becomes increasingly an issue in modern literature. In the 20th century man is reduced to a cockroach, as you will find when you read Kafka's Metamorphosis. The work is so dehumanizing, that Gregor becomes an insect, and we identify with him in ways that quite surprise us. So Voltaire's vision is optimistic, not pessimistic at all. He says that in this meaningless, crazy world we are able to fashion meaning out of our action, and work becomes the salvation. Deeds not words are all-important. ♣

Now, please enjoy the videotape.

IV. REVIEW QUESTIONS

1. Does <u>Candide</u> offer any alternatives for what it tears down?

2. What exactly will we accomplish by cultivating our own garden?

3. Is Eldorado a utopia? Why? Is it perfect? Would you like to live there?

4. What is the role of Cunegonde in the story? Martin? Jacques? Pococurante?

5. What does Voltaire imply about Providence or the role of God in earthly affairs?

V. FURTHER READING

Aldridge, A. <u>Voltaire and the Century of Light</u>. Princeton, NJ: Princeton University Press, 1975.

Wade, Ira O. <u>The Intellectual Development of Voltaire</u>. Princeton, NJ: Princeton University Press, 1969.

Wade, Ira O. <u>Voltaire and "Candide:" A Study in the Fusion of History, Art, and Philosophy</u>. Princeton, NJ: Princeton University Press, 1959.

NOTES

LESSON 18:   GOETHE, FAUST

 Before you read this chapter of the Study Guide

READ: Text: Maynard Mack, Ed., Norton Anthology of World
Masterpieces, vol. 2, pp. 464-569

I.   INTRODUCTION

I think it's fairly safe to assert that <u>Faust</u> is the most difficult and least accessible work you will read in this course. Its language is difficult, its structure can be confusing, and its ideas can sometimes seem elusive. Having said all that, I think the play is important both as a representative text of European Romanticism and because it raises essential—albeit difficult—questions that we still wrestle with: how can we best integrate the demands of head and heart, how do we reconcile desire with responsibility toward others, how do we best find personal fulfillment?

How best to read <u>Faust</u>? Although it may be heresy to some, I'd recommend reading it for the first time not as a play but as a philosophical poem, that is to say, focus on the language, the characters and the ideas of the text rather than on how these things are objectified for performance before an audience. In short, don't attempt a production of the play in your imagination as you read. Be a slow and careful reader of the text, paying attention to the particularly dense and rich metaphors, the long set descriptive pieces, the way dialogue fixes characters in the play. Don't read it as producer, director or actor. Save that for subsequent readings.

I urge you to pay particular attention to the Prologue in Heaven—it is central to understanding the philosophical terms of the play, the relation between Faust and Mephistopheles, and the divine favor which gives moral coloration to Faust's quest. That Faust will win his wager with Mephistopheles is never in doubt; nor is the fact that Faust's quest is a good one. These are established in the Prologue. The real question for you is the same question that God and Mephistopheles debate in the Prologue: what is the essence of human nature that Mephistopheles just doesn't get?

II.   VIDEOTAPE SYNOPSIS

The discussion focuses on <u>Faust</u> as representative of European Romanticism—its stress on individualism, limitless aspiration, gothicism, attitude toward knowledge, and so on. Particular attention is paid to the "two souls inhabit my breast" speech and the grasshopper image as emblematic of Faust's personal and philosophical dilemma.

III.   VIDEOTAPE COMMENTARY

I suggest you read this section before you watch the videotape. You will find that it will help you organize your thoughts in a more useful way than if you just watch the tape "cold." When you have finished viewing the tape you may want to read this section again.

In this lesson we take a big jump from Voltaire to Goethe, from the Age of Enlightenment to the Romantic Age. As usual I begin by asking for impressions or observations from the class. Peter observes that in comparing Candide to Faust, Faust declares that his happiness is the pursuit of it.

Valeria sees Faust as steeped in academia, but he wants to experience sensual pleasures before he gets too old. It's what Carl Jung would call a mid-life reversal.

I agree that Faust is a man who has trafficked only in words as the play begins, and then realizes there is an enormous gap between words and what they represent. And he has a desire for much more than what his intellect can bring to him. It is a frontal assault on the Age of Enlightenment, which put reason and logic at the center. Barbara M. makes the comparison of Satan's striking a bargain with God, just as he did in Job. The difference she sees is that Job never renounces God. I agree that the Prologue in Faust is essentially modeled on the prologue in Job. There is the same kind of dramatic irony, because we know from the beginning that Mephistopheles will not be successful. (By the way don't you find Mephistopheles to be a wonderful character? He has absolutely great lines.) We also know from the Prologue that this kind of divine compassion for the nature of man is given a sanction that is tolerant of what Faust will do during the course of the play, because he knows that that spark that is in man will eventually lead him back. But that doesn't happen until Part Two, although we see the process in Part One. It begins in Part One with the love of Gretchen (or Margaret depending on your text). I hope you can also see the Miltonic echoes.

We then go on to discuss the role of knowledge in the play. Barbara M. sees an analogy with the tree of knowledge in the Bible and man's fall. I then refer to Goethe's famous predecessor, Christopher Marlowe of the Elizabethan theater. For Marlowe, Faust is an object lesson in limitation. It is the tragic history and damnation of Faust. What Faust wanted is knowledge that has been denied to man and to use it to a dark end. He is punished for it. It is an authoritarian age. It's an age of obedience. When we come to Romanticism, we find a primacy of self, it's as if the third person is replaced with the first person pronoun, the "I" comes to the fore. We don't only want to know the thoughts of the individual, but also the feelings of the individual. Feelings and emotion become very important in the Romantic Age. In the Age of Enlightenment we are cautioned to be careful of those feelings. In the Romantic Age those feelings are seen as a vehicle to a higher truth. These are very similar feelings to our own.

I remark that Goethe's Faust is a hero in the true romantic sense of the word. He is willing to break free of bounds, no matter where it leads him, either to salvation or damnation. If you are typical of first readers of Faust, you probably do not like Faust for what he does to Gretchen in Part One, but you should know that he will be redeemed in Part Two.

Virginia remarks that she felt that Faust was being used as a tool to an end. Mephistopheles thought he knew Faust's mind, but he still had a lot of goodness within him and to reach his desires he wasn't about to do other people in to achieve them. As I remark, the wager is all, because it sets the contest. It is not a play about forbidden knowledge, as in Marlowe's Faust. Goethe's Faust doesn't want any more knowledge as he has had all the brain can handle. In fact, he is contemplating suicide, as if he is lost in a dark wood.

At this point, I ask the question, What is Faust's nature? Virginia sees him as someone reaching out for his own humanity and others, although I remind her that this was at the expense of Gretchen. Valeria remarked that he didn't lack for candidates, other than Gretchen.

I then ask what the class thought of Faust, did they find it a tough read? Most agree with this. And then I ask my key question, what is it about? Eric ventures that in the first part Faust's soul is engaged in the life of the senses, in a reaction against the dryness of the scholarly life and he is plunged into an affair with a young woman. I agree that the wager is for the soul of Faust, and ask what is it going to take for Mephistopheles to win?

Susan offers that Mephistopheles wants Faust to say he is satisfied. Valeria adds that Faust is actually taking a great risk, as he doesn't know that he will be saved. He is willing to make this pact for sensual pleasures. I then ask what is Faust's problem? Virginia surmises that he is estranged from the world, he knows he is lacking something. Now he has discovered more than he can handle. He is lacking human contact, he wants to be like others. He's also aware of his age too, he's getting old. Phyllis adds that he wants to bring some mysteries to light. He ends up biting off more than he can chew. As Susan says, his feelings are not as well developed as his intellect. This is precisely where I am trying to lead the class. When Faust is on the verge of suicide something in him responds to the church bells which he remembers from childhood. This is a really important romantic idea, that childhood is a special time, a time of authenticity, that we lose as we become adults. He is literally saved by the Easter bells.

"It's not words, it's deeds." Mephistopheles, however, is the very embodiment of non-doing, despair, weakness. Chad makes an analogy with Dante. At first Virgil, the embodiment of reason, was Dante's guide, but it could take him only so far. Faust is following a similar path. His reaction to the bells is not logical reason, but something more primal. I agree that Faust doesn't need a guide. Mephistopheles is not really a guide, he does make the Gretchen episode happen, but even in Part One Faust recognizes his responsibility for the Gretchen episode. In the second part Faust picks up on his awareness and willingness to accept responsibility for Gretchen. Barbara reminds us that he says that man is made up of the carnal and the spiritual. I agree that that's classic romantic despair, to be aware that you are limited by your senses, and yet you have within you a spark of divinity.

Next we talk about Gretchen. I ask the class what they think about her. I refer to the "Sturm und Drang" (storm and stress) movement in German romanticism in which Gretchen was a type. She was the sinlessly sinning girl and her fate is just awful. I ask the class if they found her sympathetic. Virginia felt that she was really set up by Martha, who made it so easy for her. Here was someone flattering her, knowing her vulnerable spots, and she had no mother to protect her. When Faust sees her shrinking from the revelry on the mountainside, he shows guilt for what happened to her. She felt that they were both tools. Ada, however, felt that Gretchen to some extent contributed to her downfall. She showed willingness when she took the second sack of jewels and hid it from her mother. She went to Martha knowing what would happen there. I agreed with her adding that probably the most painful scene in the tragedy is Valentine's response to his sister. Virginia said that this reminded her in many ways of Ophelia. I say that this is a good analogy to make, because many of the songs Gretchen sings in Faust are based on Shakespeare's songs from Hamlet. But Ophelia is less in control of her fate than Gretchen is, and therefore more innocent.

Phyllis now brings up an interesting point. She sees part of the tragedy, not in their being enamored, but in their separating. They cannot see how the carnal and spiritual work together. As I remark, Phyllis has plugged into one of the dichotomies embedded into our Western civilization with which we wrestle profoundly. This is the notion of reason and emotion being seated in two different places and played out in two different ways. It is the classic "Cogito ergo sum" (I think therefore I am) dictum. There is no synthesizing at all. In the Western world we continually make that dichotomous decision between our head and our heart.

Ada adds that Faust represents reason and Gretchen emotions, and that they need to have both. Barbara reminds us that Voltaire warns us about reason, that too much reason will get us into trouble. As I remark, Milton said the same thing in Paradise Lost, "Be lowly wise!" There was that sense that the best use of reason was to teach you how to live well. That's exactly what Tartuffe is about.

I then ask another key question: why is Faust a hero? Usually what you have in classic heroes is that they are saying something about us that is permanent, they usually sum up certain virtues, certain qualities of character that are important, such as Oedipus's integrity, or Aeneas's characteristics of "virtus" and "gravitas." But what are Faust's principles?

Virginia sees Faust as having a sense of responsibility. For instance, when he wanted a forest of linden trees belonging to an old couple, he wanted to give them another property. He didn't want to cheat them out of anything. Susan wonders whether he might want to alter his paradigm. His has been a scholarly, intellectual existence, he now senses there is more to it than that, but he doesn't know what it is. He's a hero because he then acts on that, and he starts walking toward it even though he doesn't know what it is. Many of us would like to do this, but how many of us actually do?

I agree. At the heart of this tragedy is an awareness, as we all have two souls, we're like the "grass-hopper," Mephistopheles says, that is able to walk but is also capable of flight. We are able to take those short flights. We are aware that there is something more out there and it takes courage to leave the study and have as your only guide Mephistopheles, unlike Dante who lived in a much more stable time and who had a guide like Virgil to lead him. When we come to the post-Industrial Revolution all those old paradigms have collapsed, and the only guide Faust has is Mephistopheles, the cynic, the non-doer, the naysayer. His real guide is his own personal autonomy. He's been told that study will bring him to truth, but he learns this is not true. He also learns that religion doesn't lead him to truth either. As Phyllis remarks, Faust is really cultivating and widening his own garden, and going beyond his own plot. I follow up on this point, stating that Faust's study has widened; rather than using the books in his study, he is using the book of nature, the traditional avenue to divinity. It is through the created world that you can arrive at divinity. What Faust does for the first time, and what Mephistopheles is unable to do, is to break through his ego and find the quality of another self. Do you remember the exchange between Martha and Mephistopheles? "Are you married or are you not married?" Mephistopheles dances around the answer. He could never be married because he could not recognize the existence of another self, he is trapped within that "I." That's why Gretchen's love is redeeming. Love is creative, it is not negation. Mephistopheles stands for everything that is not love. Faust is truly a larger man at the end of Part One. ♣

 *Now, please enjoy the videotape.*

IV. REVIEW QUESTIONS

1. What is the function of the Prologue in Heaven? What do you learn about Providence? How are God and Mephistopheles characterized?

2. Discuss Faust as a prototypical Romantic hero.

3. Why is Faust in such despair about his life? What causes him to forego his imminent suicide? Is this thematically important?

4. What does Gretchen mean for Faust? How would you characterize Faust's role in courting her? How would you characterize his treatment of Gretchen? Has she any reality for him other than as an object of his sensual desires?

5. If Part I of Faust is a tragedy, what makes it so? Whose tragedy is it?

V. FURTHER READING

Atkins, Stuart. Goethe's Faust: A Literary Analysis. Cambridge: Harvard University Press, 1964.

Brown, Jane K. Goethe's Faust: The Germany Tragedy. Ithaca: Cornell University Press, 1986.

Hamlin, Cyrus. Faust. New York: W. W. Norton and co, 1976.

Mann, Thomas. Doktor Faustus. Stockholm: Bermann-Fischer, 1947. (Mann uses the Faust story to pillory Hitler's Third Reich.)

Reed, Terence J. Goethe. New York: Oxford University Press, 1984.

NOTES

LESSON 19:   FLAUBERT, MADAME BOVARY, PART 1

 Before you read this chapter of the Study Guide

READ: Text: Maynard Mack, Ed., Norton Anthology of World
Masterpieces, vol. 2, pp. 889-1120

I.   INTRODUCTION

One of the great joys of reading nineteenth-century novels is their ability to create a "world" which we vicariously enter with ease and with great pleasure. Indeed, that world is so "real"—peopled as it is with characters we instantly recognize no matter how idiosyncratic, story lines with which we can easily identify, and carefully detailed settings as seemingly familiar as our own living rooms—that we as readers can lose sight of the fact that we are reading a piece of fiction. Madame Bovary is just such a novel, one to which we easily say with Flaubert, "Madame Bovary, c'est moi."

Read the novel slowly and carefully. Don't be in a hurry. Take the phone off the hook, get comfortable and lose yourself in it for several hours. It will offer you unforgettable rewards. The novel is so beautifully written that the very act of reading it is one of its chief pleasures. If you've never had such a relationship with a novel before, then Madame Bovary will certainly become a significant part of your inner landscape.

Madame Bovary is, of course, probably the most famous French novel ever written and marks a milestone in the history of the genre. Its exceptional qualities include a style that is restrained yet poetically vivid, a setting that is so detailed and realistic and so "foregrounded" that it becomes another character in the novel, a probing of the psychology of character that results in personalities that strike the reader as utterly life-like, and a slowing down of the plot and an "internalizing" of the action that the novel as a form had not seen before. And it is all told from a point of view of disinterested objectivity which creates the novel's essential irony. As Flaubert wrote, "The author, in his work, must be like God in the Universe, present everywhere and visible nowhere."

We move from romanticism to realism, which becomes one of the dominant literary and artistic movements of the 19th century.

II.   VIDEOTAPE SYNOPSIS

The discussion centers on realism in Flaubert and Flaubert's use of "point of view" in Madame Bovary. Was Flaubert a feminist, or at least sympathetic to women's concerns? Is this novel evidence of that concern? Is the story about Charles or about Emma? Would Emma ever be satisfied with any man? If the novel has some kind of moral center, why does Charles suffer so much? Did Flaubert want the reader to be sympathetic to Emma? Are we meant to judge Emma or to understand her? Is Emma a victim of fate or circumstances, as so many say in the novel? Is she a victim of bad luck? A victim of her convent upbringing? In short, to what extent is Emma herself responsible for her own downfall? Is the novel meant to be instructive?

Video interview with:
Dr. Alison Finch, Jesus College, Oxford

III. VIDEOTAPE COMMENTARY

I suggest you read this section before you watch the videotape. You will find that it will help you organize your thoughts in a more useful way than if you just watch the tape "cold." When you have finished viewing the tape you may want to read this section again.

A. *Initial class discussion*

As usual I begin the class by asking the students for their observations. Valeria comments that you could get into the mind of a woman. Flaubert described her very well, her emotional state, her dreams. I concur, saying that in 19th century literature we're going to see the psychology of the characters, not the action, but what created the action. One of the joys, or frustrations, of this novel, is how he portrays the inner landscape, rather than the outer landscape, of his characters through Emma's point of view. Novels before Flaubert gave you lots of incidents, but Flaubert really slows the movement of the novel down, which is one of his contributions to the novel form.

Susan finds it a very sad novel. Emma had a loving husband, a daughter. She had everything she should have needed. But the two of them, husband and wife, had entirely different views on their relationship. Barbara C. also finds the novel sad. She felt that Emma was a manic-depressive, she had peaks and valleys, for which there's no solution except medication, which was unavailable at the time, so she was in a trap. I'm glad she brought up this metaphor of disease. As we move into the 19th century, the metaphor changes from sinfulness and devil possession to disesase.

Virginia brings up the subject of Charles. She felt sorry for Charles. He wasn't sure of his limits, his own abilities. People are still going to pharmacists who have no qualifications as opposed to going to him, the doctor. No one will miss him. His character was very strongly built. I agree. I point out that the novel uses the framing device of Charles. The first Madame Bovary is not whom you think it is going to be, it's Charles' first wife. We have a very slow opening, told by a narrator who uses the first person plural, "we." But the point of view shifts imperceptibly. We begin and end with Charles. It's every bit Charles' story, according to some readers. Look at his fate, it really is awful.

At this point we turn to Emma. Is she responsible for her fate? Some people say "Fate willed it that way." Remember when she and Rodolphe break up, Charles says it was fate or destiny. What is fate? What does it mean to be the victim of fate or circumstance? These are large questions of the 19th century novel. Valeria feels that Flaubert denigrates Emma, to project the male ego, his own ego, onto Charles. But as I respond, what Flaubert has in his mind he projects onto Emma, "Madame Bovary c'est moi." It has been argued that Flaubert is wrestling with his own romantic nature. I refer the class to Faust, where two souls inhabit the breast, and state that we are watching this in this novel. Emma, unlike everyone else in this provincial milieu, at least has a subjunctive sense that there is something beyond the petty, crass, clichéd perception of life.

I ask if this is a criticism of Emma and her dreams, or a criticism of the bourgeoisie that crushes a person like Emma? Susan remarks that Charles refuses to see any wrong in her, and she refuses to see any good in him. She's irritated by his almost worship of her. They really had no relationship, they were blind to each other. Emma is self-absorbed. I remark that this is one of the enduring themes in 19th century literature. People put in groups cannot connect or communicate with each other. We'll see the great example of this in Metamorphosis.

I then ask the question: if Emma is punished for her sins during the course of this novel, if suffering is the consequence of sin and error, can we conclude that reward is the consequence of something good? Who suffers in the novel more than Charles? What did he do to deserve it? Bertha is going to be sold into virtual slavery and what did she do? Charles views Emma in a way that we don't, because we are looking at her through Flaubert's consciousness. Charles doesn't have that perspective. He's an innocent, he's dull, commonplace, unromantic, but he projects his innocence onto Emma. When Rodolphe offers the horse again, Charles isn't threatened.

I share with the class that although Flaubert was seen as a pornographer by some, provincial women wrote Flaubert letters, saying "How did you know?" feeling the same sense of suffocation. Ada felt that Emma was living in a male dominated world. She makes the choice to settle for Charles, as she doesn't have many suitors. Chad felt that at least initially she was enthused about getting married to Charles. I caution the class that we really don't know this, because the scenes at the farm are seen through Charles' perspective. But we do know when the decision is made, she endorses it with enthusiasm, but she does it always in terms of clichés. She wanted a torch-light wedding, those things that she read about. She's in love with the idea of marriage, but her expectations of marriage are quite romantic and naive. And when the reality of marriage sinks in, there is that wonderfully symbolic scene, when she throws the wedding bouquet into the fire. That dry old bouquet goes up in flames. Susan remarks that it was several years before they had a child, asking if that may not have been normal. I don't know the answer to this, the novel doesn't give any clues. What is touching, however, is Emma's wanting a boy. Even then it is a stereotypical cliché, she wants a man because a man has passions that can be expressed, whereas a woman can't express them.

B. Interview with Dr. Alison Finch, Jesus College, Oxford

I begin by asking her about point of view, remarking that we begin and end with Charles, with Emma at the center, yet the point of view floats way above all of these characters, above everything. Dr. Finch responds that one reason that we begin with Charles is for purposes of dramatic suspense. We know that the novel is going to be about a Madame Bovary, but she doesn't appear for quite some time, and when she does appear, we don't see into her head. Starting with Charles is a time-honored dramatic device to make us see just how ruthless Emma is going to be. However, once we do start to see inside Emma's head, a curious double-bind in the style takes over, which indeed makes for the richness in Madame Bovary and which Flaubert is famous for, in that her thoughts are clothed in a more beautiful language than she herself could possibly have used. And yet those thoughts are constantly undercut by irony, even the prettiest of the pictures she makes for herself cannot be thought of as having any more than second-hand beauty. Flaubert is not visible in the work, as he himself said, but he is present everywhere, shaping our reactions, shaping the mixed way that we respond to Emma's thoughts. The irony is all important. He is a supremely ironic novelist, that is one of the great sources of enjoyment in the novel. The irony creates a tonic feeling, a kind of zest, seeing the lid lifted on so many phony ways of thinking.

I then ask whether Madame Bovary is a particularly modern novel? Dr. Finch responds that in fact Madame Bovary started modernism in all kinds of areas. Particularly of course the novel, in that we have a slowing down of the plot, intensive patterning inside of the novel, a deliberate attempt to set up symmetries far more focused on metaphor, far more emphasis on metaphors than one had seen in earlier 19th century novels, an internalizing of the action, and a stress on subjectivity (not foregrounded in earlier novels). We can see later famous novelists, like Proust, Gide, and the new novelists of the post-war period in France, owe a great deal to Flaubert. It's inconceivable that Proust could have written his novel if it had not been for Madame Bovary.

My next question is whether she considers Madame Bovary to be a great novel. She replied that she does, although she wouldn't want to put it way ahead of other great 19th and 20th century French novels, but she considers it one of the world classics. It's a great novel for the style it's written in, the sheer mastery of language.

C. Final class discussion

Barbara swings the discussion from the book to Emma herself. She sees her as unsatisfied in life, but a sensual person. She can never be satisfied. In the church she enjoyed the hour with the nuns; the passion, the awesomeness of it, but she couldn't stand the discipline. In life too, when she couldn't have the wedding she wanted, or she couldn't buy all the baby clothes she wanted, she lost interest in the baby even before it was born a girl. When we talk about lack of communication, she lays the blame for that on her shoulders rather than Charles's, because she could have made the marriage work but she was turned off.

I then ask what is the lesson here? That we should lower our standards? And not want romance as the world just crushes it, as romance doesn't last? Are we meant to judge Emma, understand her, or neither? Or are we to simply observe this kind of Emma? I then ask, even if Emma came to some self-awareness where could she turn and what could she do? She turns to the parish priest in a moment of crisis, to what is traditionally the moral, intellectual, and psychological center of the little village, but he is no help to her whatever. If she were a man or creative she probably could have transcended that milieu, but she is neither of those things. Can she turn to her husband, who sees nothing? She could run to the nearest city. From the end of the 19th century to the present day, we have a great movement into cities. In American literature, myths and culture, we learn that the cities are dangerous and sinful. We lead purer lives in cycle with nature from outside the city. It's a rather romantic view. One of the things that Flaubert is doing is showing us the milieu in which Emma operates; setting becomes foreground, which no one has done before. When I ask you what this story is about, you may say Emma, but you realize this is incomplete because the novel is about so much more than this individual character. What I find fascinating is, if there is dramatic tension in the novel, is it character versus character? The dramatic conflict is between Emma and her environment.

Susan adds that the environment is never more important than the scene where Rodolphe and Emma are watching the agriculture fair. You hear the hawkers, echoing and even going ahead of Rodolphe. I agree. This is one of the great scenes in literature. As Rodolphe is coming closer to the actual seduction of Emma the prefect is talking about manure!

Phyllis asks if anyone has ever met a person like Emma Bovary? It's a hungry personality. It's painful to watch and hard to be around. Susan suggests that Emma was incapable of recognizing what she had. Many of us like her stay discontented with what we have and that's tragic. I agreed that she had articulated that very nicely, because we can all say "Madame Bovary c'est moi." The key is how does one learn to live without the spark of the ideal which has formed us. Emma is singularly incapable of giving up that dream of the ideal. What is particularly crushing for Emma is that dream of the ideal is so clichéd, it's so stereotypical. Ada is less sympathetic. She doesn't see Emma as having much sense. For instance, she took all that money to flee to Leon in the city and take music lessons. She took her provinciality with her to the city. She doesn't have any tools. Phyllis however counters by saying that one cannot put one's dreams on someone else. She is a tragic figure. She has a sense of what she wants, but she can't picture it. She can only follow it. I tend to side with Phyllis, cautioning the class to be careful of judging those who do not achieve their dreams. One of the central points of the novel is that orthodoxy keeps people from experiencing life. It becomes a filter through which they observe their setting and their fellow person. Flaubert suggests that orthodoxy can be suffocating for us as it is for Emma.

 *Now, please enjoy the videotape.*

IV. REVIEW QUESTIONS

1. Do you identify with Emma or do you distance yourself from her? How do you view Charles? Is he a "good" man?

2. Is the story about Charles or Emma? If the novel is about Madame Bovary, why does it start with Charles as a schoolboy?

3. The novel begins with the narrator speaking as though he himself were in the classroom when Charles Bovary enters. He then seems to disappear from the story. What's going on here?

4. Is Emma a victim of fate or circumstances, as so many say in the novel, especially Charles? Is she a victim of bad luck? A victim of her farm and convent upbringing, which is to say, her "girlish," childish illusions about life and love? If so, to what extent is she herself responsible for her own downfall? Where, in short, does blame lie in this novel?

5. Are we meant to judge Emma or to understand her?

V. FURTHER READING

Auerbach, Eric. Mimesis: The Representation of Reality in Western Literature. Trans. Willard Trask. Princeton: Princeton University Press, 1953.

Bart, Benjamin F., ed. Madame Bovary and the Critics: A Collection of Essays. New York: New York University Press, 1966.

Brombert, Vincent. The Novels of Flaubert. Princeton, NJ: Princeton University Press, 1966.

Cortland, Peter. A Reader's Guide to Flaubert. New York: Helius Books, 1968.

Levin, Harry. The Gates of Horn: A Study of Five French Realists. New York: Oxford University Press, 1963.

NOTES

LESSON 20: FLAUBERT, MADAME BOVARY, PART 2

 Before you read this chapter of the Study Guide

Rᴇᴀᴅ: Text: Maynard Mack, Ed., Norton Anthology of World
Masterpieces, vol. 2, pp. 889-1120

I.   INTRODUCTION

It is important to say here that in a mere two hours we have only scratched the surface of Madame Bovary. The novel's extraordinary vitality is that it encourages our own private dialogue with it. Most of you will find that you will carry the novel with you—especially the character of Emma—for the rest of your life. I encourage you to re-read it occasionally as you get older. You will find the novel to be somewhat different each time you read it. Of course, it is not the novel which is changing but the reader—which is really to say the same thing.

II.   VIDEOTAPE SYNOPSIS

We continue our examination of the novel in this lesson, tightening the focus of our discussion to several important questions: how and why Flaubert manipulates the narrator's point of view to achieve irony, how gender roles (and Flaubert's explosion of several stereotypes) function in the novel, whether or not Madame Bovary is a feminist novel, and whether or not the novel communicates a clear and unambiguous moral.

Video interview with:

Dr. Alison Finch, Jesus College, Oxford

III.   VIDEOTAPE COMMENTARY

I suggest you read this section before you watch the videotape. You will find that it will help you organize your thoughts in a more useful way than if you just watch the tape "cold." When you have finished viewing the tape you may want to read this section again.

A.   Initial classroom discussion

As usual I begin by asking the class for questions. Virginia wonders why if Emma were able to find some satisfaction through other men, she didn't turn to Charles in the first place? Barbara C. thought that she was looking for excitement, which was not to be found in her husband.

I reminded the class of the point of view, which is the narrator's position in terms of the novel. Flaubert had to find his angle of vision for the story, which is not an easy one, because he wants you to see the milieu not just from the point of view of the participants, but a larger point of view which will allow irony. Without a larger point of view there can be no irony. He could have told this whole novel from the point of view of Emma, but how could he achieve this extraordinary irony? Emma is too limited to give an ironic detachment. Charles is the same way; he's dull, unimaginative, unobservant. So it begins with a "we," this classmate of Charles is the best we can do. Then it changes from we to a third person who looks at the farm. We then start to perceive from Charles's point of view at the farm. We get to see Emma; first it's her eyes, then the whiteness of her nails, and the sound of her shoes on the kitchen floor. Piece by piece we get a view from Charles. Subtly the point of view changes and we move from the outside in. The real drama is occurring between the ears of Emma. The imperceptible shift is from Charles to Emma. Interestingly enough even as we see through Emma, and she is so limited, we need yet another voice. And that's the narrator up here. And it's that distance between Emma and the narrator that achieves the irony. As Dr. Alison Finch said, if we see through Emma the language will be flat and prosaic, but Flaubert gives you an extraordinarily vivid style through his point of view. When we get into the novel, the perspective shifts yet again to the outside. We're left with an epilogue, rather than a climax, of Charles's death.

Virginia persists, and wonders whether Emma could not have made her wishes known to Charles and gone with him straight to a big city. I remind her of the scene where Charles finishes his rounds and comes home to dinner. Haven't you seen couples in restaurants who have been married for a long time and have nothing to say to each other? Emma is then aware that she cannot connect with Charles. As Valeria remarks, his very contentment exasperates her. Susan adds that on the night of the wedding we assume that Emma is a virgin. However, Flaubert says that after the wedding night it seems to be Charles who has lost his virginity. I remark that Flaubert plays with the notion of gender frequently in the novel. When we come to the end of the novel, it's Emma seducing Leon. And Emma becomes the man in the relationship and Leon is the traditional female in the relationship.

We now consider Charles. Is he good? As Emma says at the end, with one of her last words, "Oui, tu est bon." Barbara C. thought that one of his failings is being unable to see into his wife and knowing that she was unhappy and not knowing how to make her happy. Pat felt that Charles was a nice man, but not necessarily good. He needed to be a larger man. Emma was bored on the farm and Charles was a way of escape. But he was just as boring. It was a lack of his ability to dream her dream, or provide an intellect for her to reach for, which made it impossible for him to help her. Peter felt that one of his faults was that he always chose an easy path. His father pushed him along. He didn't become a true, full-fledged doctor. He was pushed into operating on Justin's leg. He wouldn't have thought of it or done it on his own. I concur: Charles is not an ambitious man at all, and he's not going to be Emma's entrée into the world of the ball. But Ada jumped to his defense. Charles is loyal, honest, and honorable. He is everything Emma is not. At this stage I caution the class that Flaubert did not want us to judge people in his book. What got him in so much trouble with this novel is there is no authority voice, other than the ironic one, which does judge. The irony is a kind of judgment. But there is no explicit place in the novel where you can see that Emma is being punished. What is she being punished for, her adulteries? She is an untidy housekeeper, she cannot keep the books, unlike Lheureux, the shopkeeper. Barbara M. agreed that she committed suicide over the indebtedness, not because of the affairs.

I then ask how many of the class see this as a feminist novel. Is Flaubert able to view the world sympathetically from a woman's perspective? Does he capture a feminine sensibility, does he say what it is to be female? Phyllis noted that he got a strong response from women who read his novel. Elaine said that Emma wanted more than the parochial environment gave her, and in that way it speaks to feminism. Women want more than the boundaries set up by the men in society. I agree, pointing out that that's what is so terrible about Emma's fate. If she were male, she might have found ways to transcend her dilemma. But she does not have the avenues available. She can't find another kindred sensibility in that town, other than Leon. Her incompleteness is not of her making, so be careful of judging her. Even Ada conceded that as a doctor's wife in that little town, she enjoyed a special status. On that level, she had no-one in whom to confide, she had no peer.

B. Interview with Dr. Alison Finch, Jesus College, Oxford

I asked her whether she thought that Flaubert was a feminist, or at least sympathetic to a feminist point of view. Dr. Finch replied that she felt that Flaubert was a feminist, but he is also anxious to show ways in which men are not liberated. He is trying to explode stereotypes that both sexes have about each other and themselves. She cites the paragraph where Emma is exploring the reasons why she would rather give birth to a boy than a girl as extremely significant. She would like a boy because men at least are free to travel all over the world, to have as many passions as they like. She thinks women are too subject to the softness of the flesh. They are even legally restricted.

But she felt Flaubert was also trying to say that in the kind of society Emma lived in neither men nor women were free, so it might be an androgynous book. In the very characters he creates, he is anxious to show that men can have feminine traits and women can have certain masculine traits, particularly in the case of Emma's relationship with Leon.

I then asked if there were a moral in this novel. Dr. Finch replied that if there were instruction it is to be aware of ambiguity, to get away from cliché. Flaubert was very keen on exploring received ideas. He wanted to write a dictionary of received ideas. Maybe he says that we should be careful of religious and political orthodoxies, but you can see a slight leaning toward liberalism.

(The concept of "received ideas" may be unfamiliar to you. They are those ideas, attitudes, or ways of seeing the world that come to us whole cloth, based neither on our own experience nor our own reasoning. In short, they are those unexamined orthodoxies which can keep us from living free and authentic lives. Emma's ideas about love and marriages are received ideas.)

We ended by talking about Flaubert's attitude toward provincial life. Dr. Finch felt he was certainly vicious about the narrow-mindedness that one can find in the provincial clergy, the provincial scientist. I remarked that she seemed to be unlucky in being up against people like Lheureux who was out to despoil her, or the crushing stupidity of the priest, Bournisien. Dr. Finch agreed, but felt we should ask the question, was she unlucky or would it have happened anywhere?

C. Final class discussion

We take up Dr. Finch's remarks about Emma's received ideas, such as "Time, or place, will bring change for the better." But you bring this self with you as you change place. Unfortunately, she's wrong on both counts, because she's bringing that same limited perspective with her. Valeria felt that Flaubert was projecting his own feminine side onto Emma. I refer to Flaubert's letter to Louise Colet. What moves Emma is all of the sense impressions (of the ball) that bestow on the individual something meaningful. She is convinced that by changing the trappings, she can change the reality. That's nowhere better seen than with the cigar box; she is convinced it belongs to a count. It becomes a talismanic thing that bestows on her the grace and elegance that she doesn't otherwise have.

I remarked that Emma lives in a perpetual present, which is why Lheureux can spoil her the way he does. She has a childlike quality, to live in a perpetual "now." Susan wondered whether she is living in a dream, rather than having a dream. I reply that if she does have a dream, it's stereotypical, it's hardly her dream. It's as if she has edited somebody else's movies, but they are not her own. The tone of the narrator gives us the ability to distance ourselves from these characters, even as we enter her consciousness. We say this may be true of Emma, but not of us. Who of us cannot say that those orthodoxies were not foisted on us? For this novel to work it must be instructive, but not in the sense of 19th century moralism (don't commit adultery). What separates romantic art from realist art is the presence of that "I", the writer, in the work, such as in Rousseau's Confessions. He is trying to achieve an objectivity. However, if you are not aware of the narrative voice, you are not aware of irony. Because realism deals with the commonplace, it becomes something personal. Antigone and the Iliad are so much larger than life. You recognize the humanity, but there's no identification.

I then turned to the question of authenticity. I asked the class if we were to put Emma in the 20th century, would the story maintain its vitality? When I look at this novel and I look for someone who is not wrapped up in orthodoxies, not stereotypically sleep walking through life, who do I find? Homais is the bourgeois progressive, maintaining faith in science, faith in reason, faith in progress. Bournisien is at the opposite end of that debate between science and religion in the 19th century. Homais is the representative of the spirit of Yonville and the spirit of his age, the triumph of the middle class. He is totally blind to the actuality of other selves, he is an egoist. Bournisien has a religion that cannot reach out, it is wrapped up in formality, like the ball. Happiness is an invention of the devil to make people miserable. Ennui is the normal state of things and what we need to do is learn how to live with that, and not create fictions. Your dreams are nurturing, they are not necessarily destructive. Willy Loman dreams that tomorrow will be better. Phyllis sees Emma trapped and sees many of us who can identify with her in feeling trapped. Chad felt that she was only content when she was miserable. It's a source of comfort for her. She sabotages other possibilities

I state that it is very difficult to recognize the orthodoxies that you are wrapped in and it is very difficult to step outside them. Andre Gide, 40 years after Flaubert, writes about the need to go out into the desert, like Christ, as a necessary journey. The desert becomes an interesting metaphor, because there is no nurturing, it is very different from a garden. It's a metaphor for getting outside of all those old support structures, those received ideas. You have to leave the family, the school, the government. You have to win some kind of authenticity. But you also have to come back to civilization. It gets harder as you get older, because of the variety of responsibilities. The one man in the novel that she thinks she could be the most happy with is the one who abuses her the most, Rodolphe. Pat interjected that if Emma were a woman of the 20th century she would have favored yellow wallpaper! Virginia answered that Flaubert gave Emma an opportunity for contentment, by giving her a child, which could have been a saving to her. However, the baby becomes an inconvenience to her. It prevents her from learning selfless love, she is indeed selfish. It's part of the trap of the inarticulate not to know the commonality of the human experience. ♣

 *Now, please enjoy the videotape.*

IV. REVIEW QUESTIONS

1. Martin Turnell argues in <u>The Novel in France</u> (1950) that <u>Madame Bovary</u> is "an onslaught on the whole basis of human feeling and on all spiritual and moral values." Do you agree? Are there any positive moral exemplars in the novel? What do these people stand for?

2. If the novel does have some kind of moral center, why do Charles and Bertha suffer so much?

3. Flaubert seems to be a feminist, or at least sympathetic to feminism or women's concerns. Is this a feminist novel?

4. Is Emma a masochist? I'm not trying to be cute here; it seems as if the only man she would have been consistently happy with is the man who abused her the most, Rodolphe.

5. Would Emma ever be satisfied with any man? with any love?

V. FURTHER READING

Please refer to the references in Part I.

LESSON 21: DOSTOYEVSKY, CRIME AND PUNISHMENT

🖝 ***Before you read this chapter of the Study Guide***

READ: Dostoyevsky, <u>Crime And Punishment</u>. (Note: This book is not contained in the Norton Anthology of World Masterpieces) I suggest the Modern Library edition.

I. INTRODUCTION

You will be excused a certain sense of dislocation as you read <u>Crime and Punishment</u> after reading <u>Madame Bovary</u>, for they are very different novels indeed—different in scope, different in purpose, different in style and different in conception, to name but a few. One might argue that these two novels are the two poles of the novel form as it has come down to us in the twentieth century. Flaubert writes an "art" novel, highly conscious of form and the "mot juste" (the perfect word). Dostoyevsky writes a novel that seems to capture the very formlessness of life itself: so much detail, so many strange and seemingly inconsequential things happening to so many people living in so dark and irrational a world. Each author is rightfully claimed as the "father" of the modern novel.

If you are a first reader of <u>Crime and Punishment</u>, I'd suggest you read it as the good detective novel that it is. A young, impoverished student commits a "perfect" crime—nobody sees him do it and he essentially goes scot free. But then the "chase" begins, a chase very different from the one you are familiar with from movies or television. Raskalnikov runs toward his punishment rather than away from it. Having performed the "perfect crime," he starts dropping clues all over the place. And as he does so, the noose—both of his own invention and of Porfiry's, the detective—begins to tighten. The once arrogant intellectual, who could sum up all humanity in his neat theories, must learn through the course of the novel what it really means to be free and by what yardstick one measures human worth.

But read it, too, for the world of the novel. Get absorbed in it and let it absorb you. To enter a "Dostoyevskyan" world is to enter a world which baffles our ordinary perceptions. It is to be aware that there is so much more going on than what we are capable of perceiving or normally conceiving. Some have accused him of creating an "improbable" world in his novel, peopled as it is with murderers, prostitutes, sadists and masochists. To which Dostoyevsky replied that he is a "fantastic realist," by which he means that he is not concerned with the kind of reality that happens most of the time to most people. People do not show who they are in their repetitive actions. Rather, they show themselves in crisis situations—in, if you will, "fantastic" situations. That is not unreality; it is a "realer" reality through what one can call "fantastic realism." What do you think?

II. VIDEOTAPE SYNOPSIS

The discussion focuses on Dostoyevsky's unique contribution to the novel form, his interest in the obscure and confused motivations of human action and his interest in the multiple personality and the themes of suffering and spiritual regeneration. What is the "idea" behind the novel? Are the main characters of the novel embodied "ideas"? Is the "Epilogue" difficult to accept artistically or psychologically?

Video interview with:

Professor Ed Wasiolek, University of Chicago, editor of <u>Crime and Punishment and the Critics</u>

III. VIDEOTAPE COMMENTARY

I suggest you read this section before you watch the videotape. You will find that it will help you organize your thoughts in a more useful way than if you just watch the tape "cold." When you have finished viewing the tape you may want to read this section again.

A. *Opening class discussion*

I begin by asking the class what was it like moving from Flaubert's beautifully crafted novel to <u>Crime and Punishment</u>. Barbara M. replied that with Dostoyevsky there was a lot of drama, that you feel the feelings of the characters. I agree. Dostoyevsky said this is reality in the sense of capturing the human soul, the psyche. In response to Virginia's comment that everyone seemed to be helpless, I add that there is a sense here that life is stronger and has more force than the human ability to control it, shape it or make sense of it. Intellect and reason are not necessarily the motivations for human action. Rosemary makes the point that today we tend to sympathize with people who do something wrong and make excuses for their actions, such as they had a bad childhood, and so forth. As society has become more complex, there is no good or evil. It wipes away the ethics. This, I observe, is right at one of the issues in this novel. Valeria comments on Raskalnikov's theory that there are extraordinary men and ordinary men, that people like Napoleon could exceed the bounds of good behavior. He tried to apply the theory to himself and the pawnbroker, but somehow that went by the boards when he killed her. The crime seeped into his conscience without his realizing it.

I then ask one of the central questions, when you commit a crime is there a voice inside you that will insist on punishment for the crime? Peter said that Raskalnikov makes a case for superior people, whom we need, such as Lenin, Washington, and Napoleon. They make things happen. But then he balances it with the question, what would happen if you had all superior people? As I respond, what he discovers is that his little intellectual theory is exactly that, a little intellectual theory. Raskalnikov during the course of the novel discovers that he is not a superman.

I then give a little background for the novel. One of the things that Dostoyevsky is doing is attacking some of the social theories that are evolving in Russia even as he writes. As a young person he had quite liberal sentiments. He had a horrifying experience when he was arrested for these sentiments. He was taken out to be executed, blindfolded and at the last minute received a reprieve from the Czar. It wasn't until his second marriage that he became a success. He then became quite conservative in his social views later in life. Here he is attacking this notion of socialism that is starting to take shape. One of the things that makes him nervous about the socialists is they're theory-based rather than experientially-based. Now their goal is good to be sure, but he is afraid of the theorists. Barbara M. remarked that Raskalnikov said that under socialism there would be no need for crime, but she felt that they failed to take human nature into consideration.

We then discuss why Raskalnikov commits this murder. This novel is not as easy to fathom as <u>Madame Bovary</u>, it's hard to find those well springs of human motivation. Ada felt that he was similar to Emma in that he is so self-absorbed. I respond that one of the ideas of the novel is his resurrection via Sonia. He learns humility and love from her. And the wonderful irony is that he learns the highest virtues from those people that society thinks are the most disreputable, while the most reputable people in the novel are the most morally abhorrent.

Virginia adds that throughout the whole book so many things happened because the women supported the men. Raskalnikov's sister was willing to marry a man whose family had been so terrible to her family, whom she had met once. Pulkheria Alexandrovna gave to her son everything, so she had nothing for herself. Women sacrificed for the men. I agree. This novel will demonstrate for you the downtrodden lives of women in 19th century Russia. Some of the male characters have will, in the sense that they can exercise their energy on the world, but the women are truly at the mercy of the men that surround them. Sonia becomes a kind of Beatrice in the novel.

We then turn briefly to the epilogue, which Virginia has touched on. I confess that I have real trouble with the epilogue, I think it's not terribly well prepared, it is entirely too neat. There is no subtlety at all. It's too rapid of a conclusion. Obviously the lesson to be learned here is that through his suffering in this warfare, if we can come back to the idea of the devil, Raskalnikov struggles between the Sonia in him (the meekness, humility, and his friends commenting on his goodness) and his incredible arrogance. He has this little theory about supermen and the whole rest of humanity; it's as if the Sonia is at war with the Svidrigaylov in him. And at the end we are expected to believe that he goes off into the sunset with the Sonia in him. Valeria comments that to her the ending wasn't quick, it was natural, that it appeals to the spirituality of the Russian people, which is an excellent point.

We then take up the point of value as a human being. This was triggered by Valeria's remark that Raskalnikov saw the pawnbroker as a louse on society; she preyed on students, she was of no worth. And he says, "I killed her for myself." However, when he killed the innocent Lizaveta, his conscience bothered him. I remark that this is the difference between individual morality and social morality, where you get into defining human beings in terms of usefulness and uselessness. You get into that in the 20th century where you measure a person's worth, and that's an utterly terrifying idea. We all do this. We generally do this in terms of economics, but we also do it more and more in terms of medical ethics. Ada remarked that there is good and bad in all characters in this novel. Sonia, the prostitute, is not all bad.

B. Videotape interview with Professor Ed Wasiolek, University of Chicago, editor of *Crime & Punishment and the Critics*

Professor Wasiolek leads off the interview by stating that one can read <u>Crime and Punishment</u> like a detective story because it's a chase, a very familiar form which we see on TV all the time. The difference here is that Raskalnikov is running towards his punishment, rather than away from it. Having done the murder without implication, he then drops clues all over the place.

I ask what is Dostoyevsky's point in this? Is it that the sinner demands punishment? Professor Wasiolek agrees, adding that it is a very hard concept for us to accept. However, we have to make a distinction here, is Dostoyevsky saying that everybody has this inner voice? Or that everybody should have this inner voice? Probably the latter. And in a sense it's not so different from going all the way back to the Greeks, because Raskalnikov wanting to be punished is in a sense learning from suffering. So it's a familiar idea with a modern twist. Why do we have to suffer? First of all, Raskalnikov begins with the arrogance of youth, the arrogance of the intellectual, and how do you get out of that? By personal suffering. Collective suffering is always abstract.

Professor Wasiolek then turns to the problematic ending. It's not troublesome that Raskalnikov should have come to a reconciliation by way of suffering and by way of the intercession of Sonia. This is a kind of rebirth. We see the reverse of the callous, young intellectual that he was. That is done very well, because of the psychological probability, and it is done slowly with the whole drama of resistance on his part. What offends us is the rapidity of the end.

Finally I ask what does Raskalnikov learn from Sonia? Is it a lack of ego, a kind of submissiveness, that is burned out of him? Professor Wasiolek replies that one of the central ideas of this novel is freedom, quoting from Dostoyevsky's short work, <u>Notes from the Underground</u>. The premise for this book is one that runs through all of Dostoyevsky's works, expressed in <u>The Brothers Karamazov</u> as "If God doesn't exist, all is permitted." Raskalnikov says, "I can do anything because I can kill a useless pawnbroker." But what he discovers is that he has a false freedom. Sonia represents a true freedom. Why? In the West, freedom is the ability to do one's will. But Sonia is the opposite. You find this idea in Russian thought, the freedom to expand inside. You become big and in a sense universal. Something is released inside of you. Sonia does it by accepting Raskalnikov who expects to be condemned by her. You accept the fact that you don't understand the world, which is a kind of force. Understanding is another kind of judgment. It is an act of will. There is a kind of freedom in will-less-ness. This is a common trend in Russian literature.

C. Final class discussion

The discussion picks up on Professor Wasiolek's notion of the different kind of freedom in the East, the Asian influence in Russia. The Western notion is that there is a world out there that is different from the self. But there is also a new perception of the self as an actor in the world. The Asian notion breaks down that perception of the world as object and the self as subject. Even other selves are objects in this novel, and the pawnbroker is an object because Raskalnikov can do things to her. What happens in the end is that the sense that he is separate from the object really breaks down. He learns love by breaking through the prison of the self, and don't miss the irony. Where does it happen? In prison.

Finally, Valeria begins a discussion of the peasants in the novel, stating that Dostoyevsky and Tolstoy were kinder to peasants than Flaubert was. I agree that there are several traditional myths in this novel. One of them is the earth and Mother Russia. The other is the notion that one learns from the peasant. The peasant embodies the pure, noble, and righteous ideas. Similarly the city is absolutely brutal in Dostoyevsky's writings. Ada adds that we feel that the peasants are unpolluted by urban problems and ideology. Because of their closeness to nature we associate them with closeness to God. Urban dwellers are considered soft in mind, body, and spirit. I agree that this is a theme from the Industrial Revolution to about 1830. There is this sense of progress, but with this you also get the growth of cities, big crowded dirty alienating cities, and this becomes a struggle of how the city becomes a kind of unnatural environment. Sonia becomes a prostitute in order to survive. You need to leave the city in order to recapture your essential human nature. ♣

 *Now, please enjoy the videotape.*

IV. REVIEW QUESTIONS

1. Many critics consider the ending of the novel to be weak. Do you think that the alternative ending that Dostoyevsky considered in his notebooks of Raskalnikov shooting himself would have been better? Defend either the present ending or the alternative.

2. Why did Raskalnikov kill the pawnbroker? Be as specific and thorough as you can.

3. How different would the novel be without Porfiry?

4. Dostoyevsky's notebooks indicate that he intended Svidrigaylov and Sonia to express two sides of Raskalnikov's character. Has he done this successfully in the novel?

5. As an epigraph to <u>The Brothers Karamazov</u>, Dostoyevsky took the words from the Gospel of John: "Except a kernel of wheat fall into the ground and die, it abideth alone; but if it die, it bringeth forth much fruit." How well does this express the theme of <u>Crime and Punishment</u>?

V. FURTHER READING

Dostoyevsky, Fyodor. <u>The Notebooks for Crime and Punishment</u>. Wasiolek, Edward, ed. and trans. Chicago: University of Chicago Press, 1967

Jones, Malcolm V. <u>Dostoevsky: The Novel of Discord</u>. London: Barnes and Noble Books, 1976.

Lord, Robert. <u>Dostoevsky: Essays and Perspectives</u>. Berkeley: University of California Press, 1970.

Rosen, Nathan. "Chaos and Dostoevsky's Women," <u>Kenyon Review</u>. XX, 1958, no. 2 Spring, pp. 257-277.

Simmons, Ernest J. <u>Dostoevsky: The Making of a Novelist</u>. London: J. Lehmann, 1950.

Steiner, George. <u>Tolstoy or Dostoevsky</u>. New York: Knopf, 1959.

Wasiolek, Edward, ed. <u>Crime and Punishment and the Critics</u>. San Francisco: Wadsworth Publishing Company, 1961.

Wasiolek, Edward. <u>Dostoyevsky</u>. Cambridge, Mass: M.I.T. Press, 1964.

Wasiolek, Edward. "On the Structure of Crime and Punishment," <u>PMLA</u>. vol. 74, no. 1, pp 131-136, March, 1959

LESSON 22:   TOLSTOY, THE DEATH OF IVAN ILYCH

 Before you read this chapter of the Study Guide

READ: Text: Maynard Mack, Ed., Norton Anthology of World
Masterpieces, vol. 2, pp. 1209-1250

I.   INTRODUCTION

When I ask students to name the most personally influential work they've read in my World Literature survey, most answer with Tolstoy's The Death of Ivan Ilych. The story of Ivan Ilych (the Russian equivalent of John Doe) packs an emotional wallop, especially since we as readers spend a considerable amount of intellectual and emotional energy—while actually reading the story!!— denying that we have much in common with this undistinguished man. All this may be true of Ivan, we say, but what has it got to do with me?

And then, perhaps slowly, we come to realize that we are responding to the story just as Ivan responded to the syllogism he learned in school: "All men are mortal. Caius is a man. Therefore, Caius is mortal." As Ivan says, "That may be true of Caius, but what has it got to do with me?" Such abstractions about death—say it several times, "All men are mortal"—rather than communicating the reality of our mortality may, instead, anesthetize us to it. What Tolstoy achieves in this story is nothing less than to make us see ourselves vicariously as a corpse in our own coffin. As we watch Ivan's fate slowly unfold before our eyes, who of us doesn't wonder if we may be watching a preview of our own fate?

Tolstoy has written a story not so much about death and dying as about how to live an authentic life. Chapter 2 begins with one of the most famous lines in all literature: "Ivan Ilych's life had been most simple and most ordinary and, therefore, most terrible." What is it about the simple and ordinary life that we should associate it with terror? Ivan on his deathbed looks back to a life lived with propriety and decorum and finds it wanting if not meaningless. As he reviews his life, the only time of real authenticity he can find is his childhood. His whole life has been "wrong." Why? And how can we as readers learn from Ivan's life so that our own can be more authentic and less anonymous and isolated?

II.   VIDEOTAPE SYNOPSIS

The discussion focuses on the story as, among other things, a "memento mori"—forcing a consciousness of death in order to force an examination of the authenticity of our lives. "Ivan Ilych's life had been most simple and most ordinary and therefore most terrible." What does this triad of adjectives mean? What is the tone of the story? Is Ivan's fate a blessing or a curse? What is the role of Gerasim? the "friends?" the family? The discussion focuses on the imagery at the end of the story as it relates to the story's theme.

Video interview with:

Professor Ed Wasiolek, University of Chicago

III. VIDEOTAPE COMMENTARY

I suggest you read this section before you watch the videotape. You will find that it will help you organize your thoughts in a more useful way than if you just watch the tape "cold." When you have finished viewing the tape you may want to read this section again.

A. *Initial class discussion*

The program opens from Eyam near Sheffield in England, where many of the village inhabitants were killed in the Plague of 1665 to 1666. It was an appropriate place to reflect on death. I remark that in the <u>Death of Ivan Ilych</u>, Tolstoy confronts us with the death of a very ordinary man surrounded by very ordinary people. A great gray nonentity slowly dies and in that process he confronts a life never lived. The role of "memento mori" (a reminder of death) is to remind us that our task is to live and to live authentic lives.

I begin the classroom discussion by asking for comments. Chad remarked that initially he thought the story was about the three characters in the beginning, but then it shifts to Ivan's story. The story begins with the ending. Barbara C. wonders about the description of the hassock, wondering if that could have been Ivan's spirit. I remark that I thought this is designed to deflate that scene somewhat, because Praskovia Feodorovna is not the most sympathetic character in the story. She does seem a little predatory. Their marriage was a ghastly one, and perhaps not an untypical one. On almost all levels, you as the reader resist this story. You both distance yourself and at the same time recognize yourself in it. As you move through the story, your defenses are ultimately worn down and you say "That's exactly the way it is."

Ivan Ilych is the representative middle-class person. He has the power to sniff out what those in positions of authority consider to be the right thing to do. Everything has to be "proper." It becomes painfully clear to him that his life has been utterly vacuous. He has played roles, he has been a father, husband, and a judge, but he has not been a self. The wonderful irony is that he receives his fateful injury decorating this pretentious house so that it would look like those of all other members of his class.

In his first chapter he implicates all of us in relationship to death. Ivan cannot connect with the doctors. He wants to know ultimate answers to ultimate questions, and the doctors are debating his appendix or kidney. Philipe Aries wrote a book called <u>The Hour of our Death</u> that traces death and dying in conjunction with culture. He says that this was one of the first works that introduces the doctor to the dying process. Tolstoy viciously satirizes the doctors; they want to debate giving the disease a name and then they may be able to do something with it. They are really missing what Ivan's real pain is, his physical pain is devastating, but what happens to him psychologically is isolating. "Oh you'll be fine" is part of that social ritual. Valeria comments that the servant recognizes that death is part of life. Ivan finally has to accept that it is happening to him. Again, I remind the class, this is the romantic view of the peasant, it's Gerasim who is quite willing to do the dirty work. Gerasim is willing to deal with him, as he regresses to the state of an infant.

Virginia remarks that his wife might have been his opportunity to become human. She was the prettiest and liveliest girl, who could have become a model partner for him. But he ignored her and concentrated on his ambition. There were chances for him to become real. However, I counter by saying that this would only happen if he recognizes that he has a self to give, and he doesn't recognize that until his own extinction. He is away at work doing that role that society assigns to him, but he is sleepwalking. All his energy to discover what causes his pain is quite beside the point, what he has to discover is much more difficult than putting a label on a disease. The irony of the sign on his watch chain is that he has carried it with him all of his adult life, and he has never once "respique finem-ed!" ("think of the end.") When he looks back over his life he realizes that it was only in childhood that he was free to be himself. Ivan looks down and notices his son, who is a little Ivan, and sees his tears. He then becomes aware of the boy and his wife in a way he has never seen them before, and he wants to say "Forgive me," but instead he says, "Forego" (Let it be).

Tolstoy doesn't give you a cheap ending. Ivan goes through forty-eight hours of enormous pain and suffering. His wife complains that it was awful for her. Dostoyevsky is a young person's writer and Tolstoy is an older person's writer, because Tolstoy gets right to the core of human experience. Death and dying has become a cottage industry in America, and Elizabeth Kubler Ross has used Ivan Ilych as an example of the stages that people go through in dying. Helen quotes from Elizabeth Kubler Ross: "When the time comes to die, it is only the love we have given or received that will make a difference. For all others, death will come too soon and be too horrible."

I ask about the ending. It is a Christian ending, to be sure, but not exclusively Christian. I ask if Ivan's fate is a blessing or a curse? Virginia offers that when he recognizes what has happened to him, it's a beginning. I concur, saying that we would all agree that he comes to a better consciousness. It occurs at the moment of his extinction, so he really doesn't have a chance to act on it, other than what he does with his wife and son, which is a kind of an act.

B. *Interview with Professor Edward Wasiolek, University of Chicago*

I begin by talking about the long tradition of "memento mori" (reminder of death) —that one doesn't live fully unless one is conscious of death. Professor Wasiolek comments that it is the consciousness of death that nourishes some of the finest emotions of human beings. Tolstoy is saying that you won't have society without a consciousness of death. The very fact that you love somebody has something to do with the brevity of time. This book is written in a period in Tolstoy's life when he is thinking about death. He is obsessive about it after his religious conversion about ten years before. He stopped writing for about ten years, between '78 when he finished <u>Anna Karenina</u> and '86. Simultaneously, you're uncomfortable with the story and yet there's a recognition there. Stylistically in Russian there is a kind of incantatory repetition of the words that Ivan Ilych lives "more pleasantly and properly". And that's exactly what's wrong with this society. Life is bigger and more complex than egotistical pleasure, it's more fulfilling if one doesn't live just for pleasure.

I then ask if Ivan's fate is a blessing or a curse. Professor Wasiolek replies that under the bludgeon of pain, Ivan is brought to a consciousness that he didn't have before. Tolstoy meant it to be better, despite the physical pain. The psychological pain comes from the nature of society and the loneliness it causes us. Tolstoy is saying that we don't control life, there are accidents. Anybody could fall off a ladder. It's how you handle it and what kind of group you live in, and what kind of emotions each person gives to the other person that are important. Finally he's even brought to compassion, for a moment he even loves his wife.

We end the interview discussing the imagery at the end, which I see as a kind of birth, rather than a strictly Christian view. Professor Wasiolek responds that conventionally, it is taken as a Christian ending. Tolstoy was developing his own Christianity at this time. There is light and there is rebirth, which is taking place on several levels, the psychological level or the emotional. Then saying "Let it be," because there is that control. Our whole society is an attempt to control the complexity of life. It is an acceptance of the world about him. It's even Freudian, the sack is a kind of reverse birth going back. Ivan regresses to a kind of childhood.

C. *Final class discussion*

Barbara M. remarked that letting go is one of the final stages in Kubler Ross's stages. Chad felt that it's very much like <u>Madame Bovary,</u> where social decorum was a sort of prison. I add that it showed the unmitigated loneliness of this poor man. Do the dying withdraw from society, or does society withdraw from the dying? The social visits stop, and the only one who continues to reach out to him is the peasant. Virginia remarks that this work seems to be very different from his other ones, such as <u>War and Peace</u> and <u>Anna Karenina</u>. I agree, saying that in this work he seems to have pared it down to essentials. As he is writing this, he is strongly committed to the moral value of literature, making it accessible for everyone. Dostoyevsky knew he would get three types of readers (hot, cold and tepid), but he wanted only passionate readers; those that loved him or hated him. Tolstoy is going for a much larger market share; he wants everybody moved by it to do what Ivan never did. He wants you to see a picture of yourself in the coffin. And if he succeeds at all it is by making you concentrate on living not dying. ♣

 *Now, please enjoy the videotape.*

IV. REVIEW QUESTIONS

1. What is the function of Chapter I? Why is it placed at the beginning of the story and not at the end?

2. Is Ivan's fate a blessing or a curse? Explain.

3. "Ivan Ilych" is the Russian equivalent of "John Doe." What qualities does Tolstoy stress in characterizing this representative of ordinary humanity?

4. Discuss Gerasim's role in the story. Is it significant that as a peasant he lives "outside" of Ivan's society? Compare him to Ivan's friends, especially in terms of his reaction to Ivan's illness and death.

5. What does Tolstoy mean when he writes, "Ivan Ilych's life had been most simple and most ordinary and, therefore, most terrible?"

V. FURTHER READING

Christian, R.F. <u>Tolstoy: A Critical Introduction</u>. London: Cambridge University Press, 1969.

Greenwood, E. B. <u>Tolstoy: The Comprehensive Vision</u>. New York: St. Martin's Press, 1975.

Matlaw, Ralph. <u>Tolstoy: A Collection of Critical Essays</u>. Englewood Cliffs, NJ: Prentice-Hall, 1967.

Simmons, Ernest J. <u>An Introduction of Tolstoy's Writings</u>. Chicago: University fo Chicago Press, 1968.

LESSON 23: KAFKA, THE METAMORPHOSIS

☞ ***Before you read this chapter of the Study Guide***

READ: Text: Maynard Mack, Ed., Norton Anthology of World Masterpieces, vol. 2, pp. 1689-1725

I. INTRODUCTION

If your first reaction to The Metamorphosis is one of bewilderment bordering on confusion, you are not alone. While your imagination will easily seize on the world of this story as some sort of hallu-cinatory experience, the narrator won't allow it. He insists that you read the story literally—"It was no dream," he says. Rarely will you have more difficulty articulating an answer to the very simple question: "What is this story about?"

And yet that very difficulty is part of the delight of reading The Metamorphosis. When we finish it, we know we have been in the presence of a compelling narrative that raises disturbing questions about our relationships to work, family and life itself. And all told in that typically Kafkaesque passionless style, as if he were a disinterested reporter merely recording the facts of a case. The tension between the extraordinary central event of the story and the very ordinary voice with which it is told makes for an unforgettable experience. Indeed, Gregor has come down to us today as a sort of cultural icon—the symbol of twentieth-century humanity in all its alienated and dehumanized condi-tion.

A dung beetle certainly is a long way from being created in the image of God, where we began this course. What about Gregor's existence would explain his waking up as an insect? How do he and the others in the story react to his new state? Are their behaviors appropriate? Is it significant that the metamorphosis occurs before the story begins? Is the story a parable of some sort? Are we to feel relief or sadness at Gregor's death?

Finally, this is what we are left with: questions which lead to more questions which lead to more. Even simple questions like positing the climax of the story are not simple questions when asked of The Metamorphosis. Perhaps Kafka has captured the essence of life in the twentieth century—the absence of old certainties, the sense of alienation and isolation, the increasing sense of vulnerability and personal smallness in the face of ever expanding bureaucracies, the terrifying notion that the center will no longer hold. Like our experience of modern life, we are left finally with only ques-tions.

II. VIDEOTAPE SYNOPSIS

The discussion focuses on the story as a modern parable, suggesting that the reality to which Gregor awakens is the truth of his life. What does this truth consist of? In what ways can Kafka's story be compared to The Death of Ivan Ilych? What is the story about? What is its theme? Where is the climax of the story? How do prose style, tone, use of detail and point of view contribute to the story's effect? To what extent does the "rage to be normal" lead us to treat those different from us as non-humans?

III. VIDEOTAPE COMMENTARY

I suggest you read this section before you watch the videotape. You will find that it will help you organize your thoughts in a more useful way than if you just watch the tape "cold." When you have finished viewing the tape you may want to read this section again.

I begin by remarking that Metamorphosis is a good introduction to the modern era, and thus a good place to stop. I ask for comments, as usual. Virginia says that for her the story is as much about the family as about Gregor. Barbara C. finds it odd that the story begins with the climax. I respond that the climax may not be in the beginning, and that we may want to look for it elsewhere. I direct the class's attention to the four chilling words: "It was no dream." It is not a metaphor. Kafka writes in a very matter-of-fact manner. The gap between the content and the form of the story creates an extraordinary tension. The matter-of-fact manner reminds Barbara M. of Voltaire's Candide, where horrible things that happened were also presented in the style of a dispassionate reporter. I agree, but add that the tone is different, because Candide had a nod and a wink, whereas Kafka wrote in a different tone.

We then explore where the humor is in Metamorphosis. Barbara C. sees it in the charwoman, her mechanical behavior is very funny. I remark that the scene with Gregor moving his little legs when he first wakes up in his new state is seen as funny by some and as terrible by others. Valeria comments that the story is appropriate for today, that workers often feel alienated, a part of the machine without ever seeing the end product. I agree that this may be a part of the theme here. Many claim that what Gregor awakes to is a sense of himself. He was not an authentic human being, but a money grubbing insect. He is a traveling salesman, which has become a metaphor in the twentieth century for the rootless, alienated kind of capitalist worker who has no place, but moves around controlled by the dictates of a possible market. Peter perceived Gregor as a terminally ill patient, which makes it gloomy for him. Barbara C. saw him as a mentally terminally ill patient, who regresses more and more into his mental death. Still on the subject of finding the humor in the book, Phyllis finds that the bizarreness of the situation is funny, but it is so in a dark way. Susan feels that Gregor never gets it. It is the ultimate stage of disillusion when he can see himself looking like an insect and yet is making plans to somehow get himself into the suit and make the later train to work. That is definitely funny, and definitely dark. One of his main thoughts is: what time is it?

I suggest that some contend that Gregor doesn't undergo any change in his life, as he has been a bug all his life. The others undergo metamorphoses in their perception of him. Chad agrees. Gregor forgets, or is not aware of, his insect-like appearance in the presence of his clerical superior. Rather he remains concerned with time, (the boss is a few minutes late). The family undergoes a change, which becomes evident in the final scene, although Kafka himself referred to the end of this story as "unreadable." Virginia and Susan mentioned Gregor's sense of obligation to the family and work. His father's indebtedness and his mother's asthmatic condition were problems that needed to be seen to. The burden of alleviating those problems was placed largely on Gregor. He, in fact, always wanted to extricate himself from that life. I suggest that he was simultaneously playing the role of the father, based on what was just said, and the newly adopted role of a child, as food had to be brought to him and he needed special attention himself. Barbara C. observed that the family functioned better when he was gone. I agree that they begin to communicate, and to function as a normal family. They clearly have a future to look forward to, but it happened at a terrible price of what Gregor had to go through. There is nothing redemptive about Kafka's story.

Mary brings up the autobiographical nature of the story. She refers to his personal letters which show that he always hated his job, as he believed that he was born to write. I agree with this. Kafka's work is seen as very autobiographical by most critics. His life indeed was one of daily clerical drudgery, which must have been all the more insufferable as it was inflicted upon a writer of such genius.

The incoherent, barely audible twitter of the roach is seen by some to parallel Kafka's own lack of opportunity to communicate his thoughts to a larger audience. Others regard this as his commentary on the situation of the Jewish community in Prague, which always perceived the rest of the society as a threat and with which its communication was limited.

Mary reminds us that Kafka had an appalling relationship with his father. I agree and note that the three scenes all end terribly. In the first one, when Gregor wants to be able to explain to his terrified superior what happened in the hope of smoothing things out, he is chased back into the room by his father with a stick. The second scene ends with his father hurling apples at his back, some of which remain lodged in it, and finally cause his death in the third scene. The symbolism of his father donning a military uniform in the second scene is hauntingly significant. Valeria points out the poignancy of Gregor's attempt to creep closer to hear the sounds of violins even at great risk to himself. I agree that this is, in his own words, the nourishment he has been seeking all his life; not the scraps of food that his sister brings him. Peter makes the point that this was almost a prophecy of the holocaust, where it is a small step from seeing somebody as a bug to treating them as one, to exterminating them. I agree, and point out that the notion of dehumanization is a constant theme in his work. Gregor's father's role was dehumanizing from the start. His mother remained affectionate, if ineffectual. As for his sister Greta, she underwent a change. After being caring, affectionate, and nourishing him both physically and emotionally, she comes to refer to Gregor as "it," and this, I think, is the climax of the story. It is not a large leap at all from that to the holocaust. Susan remarks that she has seen families both strengthened and destroyed by tragic events, especially when people are prevented by some trauma from speaking. Greta's assumption that he couldn't or didn't want to listen to her speak to him was obviously false. We should always assume that people can hear even if they cannot speak and we should communicate with them. Virginia remarks that everything Gregor did was because he thought his family wanted it. She prefers to see him as a dung beetle rather than a cockroach, as dung beetles roll little balls of dung and push them around in a rather repetitive way to fulfill their basic needs. This makes the story sad, not funny.

I remark that it doesn't take a major catastrophe in your life to turn you into Gregor Samsa. You don't need a traffic accident or a terrible disease; being caught in a nine to five job that you hate is going to do just as well. It may be just a fact of modern life that turns you into Gregor Samsa. Barbara M. observes that this is quite a fall for man, the man of Genesis becomes an insect. Phyllis remarks that there is an exit to light at the end but he is not a part of it. I state that Gregor's isolation is his own choice. He isolates himself in three stages, first to his house, then to his room, and finally, into himself. He creates his own tragedy. The tragedy of modern man is in his consciously choosing his own undoing.

"Adamah," the Hebrew word for the ground, and man made in God's own image, is reduced to the dung beetle in <u>Metamorphosis</u>. It is not by accident that we chose this work to end the sequence with. Dehumanization of those who are not like us is a 20th century notion. The family is liberated when the insect is dead. They return to normal life. Kafka was a Jew in Prague, suffered from tuberculosis and was a writer. These facts in themselves make him a victim of dehumanization of the kind that characterizes humanity, especially in the 20th century.

I point out the parallels between this work and <u>The Death of Ivan Illych</u>. Ivan at the end does come to some recognition of his self. Gregor's apparent recognition of the impending end does not necessarily amount to his understanding of the tragedy of the life that he has lead. His ultimate sacrifice is made in the face of being ignored by the rest of the family and misunderstood by himself.

Charles reminds us that this discussion is taking place in University Park, which is a new community fashioned after the original "new community," Park Forest, situated about 3 miles away, and that it was in Park Forest that William Whyte conducted his research for his ground-breaking book on alienation, <u>The Organization Man</u>. We then look at the place of literature in modern society.

The very act of taking this course is an act of stepping off the treadmill, into the uncharted land of one's own identity. It is an act which is practiced all too rarely in our world. Peter remarks that retirees who have defined themselves solely by their work have a hard time with retirement. Ada suggests that by staying within the norms, by never venturing out of them, we can all become Gregors. I agree. As a friend of mine once said: "This ain't no dress rehearsal!" If we insist on living within our boundaries, we risk failing to have an authentic life. 🎴

 ***Now, please enjoy the videotape.***

IV. REVIEW QUESTIONS

1. Martin Greenberg, a well-known Kafka scholar, argues that "The reality to which Gregor awakens is the truth of his life." Do you agree? What does this "truth" consist of?

2. What are the implications of the story's final scene? Does the ending seem appropriate?

3. Who, besides Gregor, experiences a "metamorphosis" in the story?

4. In what ways can The Metamorphosis be compared to The Death of Ivan Illych?

5. Does Gregor ever come to any understanding of the way he was exploited by his family and his job?

V. FURTHER READING

Anders, Gunther. Franz Kafka. trans. A. Steer and A. K. Thorlby. New York: Hillary House Publishers Ltd., 1960

Gray, Ronald, ed. Kafka: A Collection of Critical Essays. Englewood Cliffs, NJ: Prentice-Hall, 1962.

Pawel, Ernest. The Nightmare of Reason: A Life of Franz Kafka. New York: Quality Paperback Book Club, 1984.

Stric, Roman and Yardley, J. C., ed. Franz Kafka (1883-1924): His Craft and Thought. Waterloo, Ont.: Wilfrid Laurier Press, 1986.

Udoff, Alan, ed. Kafka and the Contemporary Critical Performance. Bloomington, In: Indiana Unversity Press, 1987.

LESSON 24:   COURSE OVERVIEW

 Before you read this chapter of the Study Guide

READ: Text: Maynard Mack, Ed., Norton Anthology of World
Masterpieces, vol. 2, pp. 1689-1725

I.   INTRODUCTION

This is the final tape in our journey of exploration of the classics and of ourselves. In this tape I ask the students to pick their favorite work from the ones we have discussed this term, and to say why they picked it. This is of course a tall order, and most had some difficulty in settling upon one distinct work. Before you read on, I would suggest that you also reflect on the works we have discussed, and pick your favorite and think about why you picked it.

II.   VIDEOTAPE SYNOPSIS

The class and I discuss the works we have read and look for common themes. There is a video insert of comments from some of our guest experts letting us know what led them to study classical texts.

III.   VIDEOTAPE COMMENTARY

I suggest you read this section before you watch the videotape. You will find that it will help you organize your thoughts in a more useful way than if you just watch the tape "cold." When you have finished viewing the tape you may want to read this section again.

A. *Initial class discussion*

Right away, I begin by asking the class, which of the works that they read this term was their favorite. Phyllis starts the ball rolling by opting for <u>Madame Bovary</u>. She cited the entanglements, the traps, the "credit card debts," the physical nature and the sensuality of it all. Her favorite line of the entire semester is when Emma goes to see Guillaumin in one of her last ditch efforts to rustle up some money. She is enmeshed in debt, on the verge of suicide but when she walks into his dining room she says, "I need a dining room like this." I agree that Emma does not have the ability to transcend the vagaries of daily life. She does not have art as a possibility. She buys those material things that represent the life to which she aspires. She really does lead a life divorced from her inner self, and yet she is the only one in that milieu with some spark of life, or poetry.

Valeria voted for <u>Crime and Punishment</u>. She relates to his theme of love as redemption, and she enjoyed the way he probed the psyche. Barbara M. liked the ironic humor in <u>Candide</u>, but she also liked the spirituality, the depth, and the universality of <u>Paradise Lost</u>. Peter preferred <u>The Aeneid</u>, saying he was moved by the story of the fall of Troy. Out of the ashes Aeneas goes on, with a great deal of self-sacrifice and a great deal of vision, to rebuild the city. He found it greatly optimistic. Virginia said that she found herself very comfortable with <u>The Aeneid</u>, the idea that driven with responsibility you proceed on. Ada's short list was reduced to <u>Tartuffe</u>, <u>Candide</u> and <u>Madame Bovary</u>. Of the three she settled on <u>Tartuffe</u>, because she liked the good laugh in the face of conventionality. Mary voted for <u>The Death of Ivan Ilych</u> because she finds it very contemporary. Chad too liked <u>The Death of Ivan Ilych</u> a lot, because he could relate to it. But he admired Antigone the most, she was just a very strong woman. She defied the will of the state for that unconditional love she had for her brother. I add that it's a strikingly contemporary play. We discussed it at a time when Nelson Mandela was about to become Prime Minister of South Africa, demonstrating the incredible power of civil disobedience.

Rosemary, to nobody's surprise, picked <u>The Book of Job</u>! I remark that Job gives us one of the threads throughout most of our works, the notion that there is this need of suffering in order for there to be a new self. Wisdom alone comes through suffering. Elaine also enjoyed <u>The Book of Job</u>. On re-reading it she saw that Job didn't suffer as patiently as she previously thought, he railed against God. It was exciting to find a new aspect. Charles noticed that most of the women seemed to like <u>Madame Bovary</u>, but his choice is the "bright star in Western literature, <u>Hamlet</u>," which he picked for the eloquence of the language and its psychological insights. Barbara M. mused that apart from Dido and Antigone, we didn't see any strong women; women were mostly ruled by their passions or by men. Valeria interjected that Eve was strong, that she defied God. I tend to agree with Barbara that so many women are portrayed as passion incarnate. Milton shows Eve as trapped, but turns her into redemptive love.

Barbara C. said her most meaningful work, not necessarily her favorite work, was <u>The Death of Ivan Ilych</u>. She found the first few pages were hard to get through, but once beyond them she couldn't put the book down. She felt for it. I respond by saying that although we called the course "Living Literature," we really picked dinosaurs. We have redefined what people read today. One of the things I wanted you to get is that they really do have a vitality, suddenly these old works just suck you in. If you allow yourself to look through Ivan's eyes, then maybe you can live your life differently. Ada adds that there wasn't one work that didn't affect her. All seemed to agree, and felt that the chance to discuss the works added greatly to the pleasure. Susan said it was hard to pick a favorite. She liked the timelessness of all of them. Every work had meaning for her. We can find a little bit of each character in ourselves. I add that writing is permanent. Each author thought that there was a need to put down those important ideas in writing. Eric just couldn't bring himself to make a choice, but observed that none of these works is as valuable as it is when it is isolated from the others. Pat picked <u>Hamlet</u>, which is the work she has read the most, but every time she reads it, she sees Hamlet in a different light. She also like the language which she found so beautiful, so changing and so alive.

B. Video-insert

I asked some of our guests in England what provoked them to dedicate their lives to these works?

Professor David Clines, University of Sheffield:

Professor Clines said from an early age that he knew that he cared about getting things right. The Hebrew in <u>The Book of Job</u> is very difficult and he felt that in choosing to work on it he was testing his strength.

Professor Zygmunt Baranski, University of Reading

Professor Baranski said that with Dante you're never bored. He really loved Dante's obsession to create this text, the richness and complexity of the work, and the way he manipulates language.

Professor Mick Hattaway, University of Sheffield

Professor Hattaway felt that Shakespeare's mind was infinitely capacious. He felt that reading and re-reading Shakespeare was for him a way of getting around the big political and cultural problems of our times.

Dr. Rachel Falconer, University of Sheffield

Dr. Falconer said that when she completed her doctorate in 1989 there seemed to be a place in Eastern Europe where the individual could contribute to history. Reading Milton sent her out to Prague, where she taught for two years, learning that history can touch the individual. As Milton exhorted, "Sally out into the dust and heat of battle!"

C. Final class discussion

Virginia now puts me on the spot; what was it she asks that drew me to study Milton? I replied that at first I just didn't get Milton, I found him as dry as dust. In graduate school I was asked to teach classical texts, and suddenly all of the reading made Milton's text vital. I was turned on by Milton's wisdom, about "being lowly wise," being out in the world, and the sheer commitment of Milton.

Barbara C. then asks me why there were no women authors. I replied that this was by design. The tendency today is to include multi-cultural aspects. I felt that this sometimes comes at the expense of covering a particular culture in depth. This kind of course is not being taught on many campuses. I tried to think of what gap to fill. I was trying to recapture the notion of the primary texts of the culture, so that one could read the multiple perspectives against that cultural background. Ada remarked that with the exception of Metamorphosis, most of these works had religious underpinnings. I reply that as we approach the 20th century, with the rise of science, you have a reduction of religion as a cultural force, whereas it was always a cultural force before. Ada responds that nevertheless the spiritual aspects of man remain predominant. I agree, adding that Dr. Wil Gaylin said that this is one of the things that defines us. What gives human beings that dignity was that subjunctive sense, the sense of the other, imagination, spirituality, aesthetics—something other than physical nature.

There's much more groping toward meaning in the 20th century. In early times there were paths laid out, and you could follow those paths toward some definite end. From the Renaissance on, we get a questioning of those paths, who laid them out, and what was their political agenda. There are some who will use the old models, but some of us won't. Alvin Toffler says we are in a third revolution, because we cannot even imagine what the future will be. There are no longer any easy answers.

Final word from the author

Perhaps we should let Jerry Garcia, late of "The Grateful Dead," have the last word for our teleclass. "What a long strange trip it's been" from Genesis to Metamorphosis! Keep on truckin', and keep on readin'! ♻

 *Now, please enjoy the videotape.*

NOTES

TELECLASS PRODUCTION

Executive Producer .... David Ainsworth

Producer/Director .... Tony Labriola

Second video producer .... Mike Griffith

Audio Production .... Jack Mulder

Video Engineers .... Ed Flowers

Bob White

Tom Sauch

Electronic Graphics .... Jacquie Hemingway

Leone Middleton

Print graphics .... Leone Middleton

Production assistants .... Patty Sue Bredesen

Jane Hu

Michael Strahl

Pilai Sukrasebya

Produced by

Communications Services

Gary Fisk, Director

A Division of the Center for

Extended Learning and Communications Services

Lee Zaborowski, Dean